## P9-AGS-488

THE

W

5-12-97

# THE
# LATEST
# EPISTLE
# OF JIM

## *Roy Shepard*

Mid-List Press
Minneapolis

FIRST SERIES: NOVEL

Mid-List Press
4324-12th Avenue South, Minneapolis, MN 55407-3218

Library of Congress Cataloging-in-Publication Data
Shepard, Roy, 1927-
The latest epistle of Jim / Roy Shepard.—1st ed.
p. cm..
"First series— novel."
ISBN 0-928811-26-1 (pbk. : alk. paper)
I. Title.
PS3569.H39399L38      1996
813'.54—dc20      96-35042
CIP

Manufactured in the U.S.A.

First Edition

This book is a work of fiction. Names, characters, places, and
incidents either are the product of the author's imagination or are used
fictitiously, and any resemblance to actual persons, living or dead,
events, or locales is entirely coincidental.

To Beth

.

# CHAPTER ONE

Few people in New Sharon could recall the day the Reverend Jack Andrews arrived. When somebody asked Lucy Shook, who lived across the street from the parsonage, whether she thought he had stayed too long, she answered that she hadn't given the matter much thought. As far as she knew, most people liked Reverend Andrews. Maybe not as much as Reverend Cruller who was more of a mixer. There was always a smile on Reverend Cruller's face. Some people liked that, although Jane Peters had told Lucy that she thought it inappropriate for a pastor to be grinning over a coffin the way Reverend Cruller did. His smile was pasted on permanently, Jane said, regardless of the circumstances. Jane had a sharp tongue when it came to ministers.

But as for Jack Andrews, he was always well-mannered and scholarly, and once you got to know him, he could be a real comfort in his quiet way. The older people especially liked having a pastor who lasted. Many couldn't remember when they had another who'd stayed as long as ten years. It was true that there were a few families, like the Hilshams who owned the Ford garage, who didn't come to church anymore. Who knew what their problem was? Car dealers were a shifty bunch. One or two people had said they thought a younger man might be better with the youth. But, on the whole, people were well-satisfied with Jack Andrews.

A few parishioners had even said that Jack was too good for the church. He ought to have a big suburban congregation, or maybe be a professor some place. His sermons were always so thought-provoking. Of course, some people liked Reverend Cruller's style more. Reverend Cruller quoted from the *Reader's Digest* and *Guideposts*, and usually ended with a poem by Edgar Guest or somebody like that. But a lot of people felt Reverend Andrews was deeper. Once there was a visitor in church—Rolland Hefner's brother from Chicago—who told Reverend Andrews it was good to hear an intellectual sermon for a change. Jack laughed and said that probably meant he hadn't made himself clear. Most sermons people thought were intellectual were not profound, he said, just obscure.

Several times lately, people had asked Lucy if she thought Reverend Andrews was thinking of moving or if he might stay on until he retired. As if she had any way of knowing. People thought that because she lived across the street she could read the pastor's mind. It was true that she did see him several times a day from her picture window. Usually he was passing between the church and the back door of the parsonage. He liked to take a short-cut through the daycare playground directly opposite where she watered her plants. Lucy showed no qualms about monitoring these frequent passages.

Reverend Andrews took it for granted that he was observed, if not by Lucy, then by others. Once, wearing those trifocals he had gotten to give himself a middle distance in the pulpit, he had stumbled into the jungle gym and barked his shin. He had fallen on one knee, and the ever-watchful Lucy had been on the verge of telephoning the parsonage to report the accident to his wife when Reverend Andrews had popped up again. He'd turned then and waved toward Lucy's window as if to let her know that he was all right. She had started to wave back, then blushed. She stood back from the window.

Wearing his dark overcoat and carrying one of his little black books, the minister was threading his way through the playground again. The Upsall funeral, of course. Lucy Shook would not be attending. She went to a good many funerals, particularly those involving people in the church, but she had never known the Upsalls or their daughter, Myra Ramsey, very well. If Myra belonged to Star or Thursday Club, Lucy might have gone anyway. But Myra did not belong to any groups except the garden club, which Lucy had resigned from when they planted petunias next to the middle school flagpole. But she knew the funeral was scheduled for Greene's at two o'clock, and there right now was one of the Greene Cadillacs pulling up in front of the parsonage door.

Reverend Andrews stopped. He stood half-turned toward the church as if caught in conflicting winds. When he saw the Cadillac, he strode briskly across the parsonage lawn, while the man from Greene's held open the door for him. One thing you could say for the Reverend John M. Andrews: When he watched where he was going, he moved with dignity.

The people who had gathered in Greene's funeral chapel sat poised for the last word. Andrews looked out over the upraised faces for a moment, then raised his hand in benediction, noting in that instant a slight movement by the dark figure who stood behind the last row of chairs.

"The God of peace, that brought again from the dead our Lord Jesus Christ, that great Shepherd of the sheep, through the blood of the everlasting covenant, make you perfect in every good work to do His will, working in you that which is well-pleasing in His sight, through Jesus Christ, to whom be glory forever and ever. Amen."

His hand came down. He picked up his book, switched off the light on the reading desk, turned, stepped down from the low platform, and walked quickly past the coffin. As he moved he could see the dark figure coming silently forward to set in motion the next stage of the proceedings.

Passing into the anteroom, Andrews paused and faced

the Tiffany. Sometimes the window looked nearly opaque, but now it glowed in the late October sun. There was no word for the wisteria that spilled a purple radiance over the archway that opened to a stone path flanked by daffodils. There was no word for that yellow, either. In the distance the pale hills ranged out of sight, beyond where he might ever go. He reached out and touched the layered glass.

The room vibrated as the organist struck up "Beyond the Sunset," and people began filing out of the chapel. He sat down in one of the flowered chairs and waited as Young Greene and an assistant ran down the hallway with baskets of flowers. A quiet feeling of elation spread over the minister. It was a feeling that often came to him on these occasions, though now, for the first time, he wondered why. In principle he disliked funeral homes. For a variety of reasons, he preferred conducting funerals in the church. Early in his ministry he had been rather stiff-necked in holding out for that. Now he was more yielding. It was one of many things that had come to matter less. And over the years, he had come to feel at home in the ancient premises of T. C. Greene & Son. The church was to be preferred, theologically and otherwise, but he had to admit that he enjoyed moving with familiar authority through the best preserved old mansion in town. He leaned back to let the pleasant feeling expand. No need to explain it. Just enjoy it. The time was past when he felt called upon to justify all his emotions.

Then he remembered the letter. This was the time he could have been reading it. He had heard the mailman coming into the church right before Millie buzzed the intercom to report that the man from Greene's was on his way. As Andrews had passed through the office, he had stopped momentarily to finger through the unsorted pile of mail on Millie's desk. It had only taken a second or two to turn up the envelope he had waited for so long. The return address was familiar enough by now. The letter had arrived. The ordeal of his temptation was no less acute because he conquered it quickly. He might have slipped the letter into his pocket for examination at such a time as this. But duty— there was no other word for it—intervened. Howard Upsall, about to be laid to rest with his fathers in the fullness of his years, deserved his pastor's undivided attention. Andrews knew that if he opened that envelope, no matter the message inside, it would hold his mind captive for the rest of the afternoon. His soul and body, too. So he dropped the latest epistle back onto Millie's desk as if it were burning his hand. Then he headed quickly for the parsonage. He knew the man from funeral home would park there; he had never been able to persuade anyone from Greene's that his place of business was the church, not his home.

Once outside, he had paused for an instant, thinking to go back and tear the envelope open. But there was the silver Cadillac. He walked decisively toward it, convinced that he had just strengthened his character with another rod of steel.

Now he wished he had shown more compassion for his own weakness. Wasn't he thinking about the letter anyway? It never paid to expect too much of yourself.

"All right, Reverend." Young Greene, in his ankle-length, oxford gray topcoat, looked in from the hallway. "We're ready to go when you are, Reverend Andrews."

He rose slowly from the embrace of the flowered chair and reached for his service book. He had laid it on the cherry dropleaf next to the glass dish with the little pillow-shaped candies. They were like ones he had known as a child, shiny in pale colors—pink, light gold, a green like that of birch leaves in spring. He reached down and placed two of the candies on the tip of his tongue. The delicate taste conjured meanings he could not grasp. Stirring himself, he moved quickly to the rack in the hallway and put on his coat.

"We can take the elevator, Reverend."

He would just as soon have walked down the maroon carpeted stairway past the other Tiffany. But the elevator, installed within the last year, was a source of much pride for Young Greene. Professional courtesy required that he take advantage of this new facility. He stepped into the elevator, followed by Young Greene and the figure who had stood in the rear of the chapel—a big man, about fifty, with a lumpy face. The pinstripes on his suit were wider than Andrews would have chosen.

Slowly they descended fifteen feet.

"Did you count?" Young Greene asked.

"I got one hundred eighteen," the assistant said.

Young Greene's face showed satisfaction. "That's about what I would have guessed," he said. "We had to bring in ten extra chairs. The daughter said only family and a few others would be there, but I knew there'd be a fairly good turnout, even if Mr. Upsall was ninety-three. It's an old family."

"And the son's somebody," the assistant said.

"That's right. Harper Wire and Cable. He's vice president, I think. Something high up, anyway. There were a couple of carloads came out from Milwaukee." He turned to Andrews and asked if he had noticed the state senator in the congregation.

"Senator Burroughs? I thought I saw him in the third row."

"That was him all right."

The elevator door opened, and the men stepped out together into the damp cold of the cement block garage that had been added on to the rear of the house. Old Greene had just sent the flower car on its way to the cemetery and was overseeing the closing of the hearse. He turned and faced Andrews. Old Greene was tall and elegant in his chesterfield. His gray felt hat set off his silver mustache. He came forward now and took the minister by the elbow.

"Nice to have the elevator for coming down, isn't it, Reverend Andrews?"

"Yes, it's a big improvement."

"A big improvement," Old Greene repeated. "Now you can ride in that car, Reverend." He pointed to a Cadillac similar to the one that had come to the parsonage, but longer. There were two rows of seats in the rear, and, as he climbed into the front passenger seat, Andrews noted that the pallbearers were already sitting in its shadowed depths.

One of them spoke: "Nice service, Reverend."

"Thank you."

Old Greene was taking his place now behind the steering wheel. "I'm glad you have that coat on, Reverend," he said. "The grave is way up on an open hillside, and the way the wind is blowing today, it's going to be mean."

It was a heavy winter coat, and Andrews had been doubtful about wearing it so early in the fall. But the only other coat he owned was a tan raincoat, which would have looked out of place, even if it had proved warm enough. He was glad now that he had taken the winter coat, despite the fact he had worn it through eight winters and it was starting to look threadbare. Though the day was bright, the wind was brisk, and Old Greene was right about that open hill.

"What cemetery are we going to?" The sepulchral voice came from the rear.

"Garden Oaks," someone answered.

"Way out there! Geez, that must be fifteen miles."

"About that," Old Greene said quietly as he maneuvered the stretch limousine smoothly and with barely a sound out of the garage and down the driveway to its appointed place: immediately behind the hearse on Clarewell Avenue. Gradually a string of other vehicles fell in behind, herded into line by the bulky assistant who stood out in the street. Andrews looked at the sign on the lawn. Its letters were gold against a background of deep blue:

T. C. GREENE & SON

SERVING NEW SHARON WITH DIGNITY

SINCE 1872

Which meant, thought Andrews, that there must have

been at least two Old Greenes before the present one.

Bo Burroughs, the state senator, had been standing next to the sign, surveying the scene. Now he moved toward the limousine, leaned forward, and tapped on the windshield until Old Greene lowered the windows.

"Nice to see you, Reverend." Burroughs reached in to shake Andrew's hand.

The minister smiled gravely. He was only a flunky in this cortege, he told himself, but the main party was hardly in a position to field such honors.

As the senator turned to leave, the assistant wearing the too-broad pinstriped suit leaned in on the driver's side. "They're all lined up," he reported to Old Greene.

"They all got their lights on?"

"I think so, but I'll check again."

In the outside mirror, Andrews watched the assistant jog along the line of cars. As he reached the corner, he turned and waved. The hearse began to move slowly and the limousine followed in what seemed like a single motion.

"Don't we have a cop leading?" a pallbearer asked.

"We should. But we don't," Old Greene answered. "There's a big funeral at St. Philomena's—that fellow fell off the scaffolding—and they're escorting over there. Told us they didn't have anyone to spare. We didn't expect many cars going out to Garden Oaks. I guess I was mistaken."

"The local cops would only take us to the edge of town anyway," another pallbearer said.

"That's right," Old Greene agreed.

The light at Willow Avenue turned just as the hearse

passed into the intersection. The great engine growling discreetly, the limousine accelerated slightly to narrow the gap. Andrews looked back to see that the others were all following in close procession. He judged that there were ten cars in all. As they left the intersection, he found himself exulting again in the sense of power that came from riding imperiously through red lights. On an opposite corner, an old man stood as if at attention, his hat removed. Flunky or not, at no other time did Andrews rise to such eminence.

"How old was Howard, Ted?" a voice asked.

"Ninety-three," Old Greene said.

"Ninety-three! God! How does a man get to be that old?"

"You gotta live right, Frank." It was the sepulchral voice again. "Stay away from cigarettes, whiskey, and wild, wild women."

"I been doing that, Herman. Not to change the subject, but, say, Reverend, when did Reverend Cruller leave?"

Andrews turned around. The speaker looked vaguely familiar. "In 1975, I believe."

The man looked puzzled. "That long? Somebody there in between, before you came, I mean?"

"There was an interim pastor," Andrews said. "I've been here over—"

"That shows how I keep up," the man laughed. "I thought Reverend Cruller was still at that church."

"We're glad you're still here." The voice came from the last row, and Andrews recognized it as belonging to a man in his congregation. "But, Reverend, aren't they likely to appoint you somewhere else before long?"

"We're free agents in our denomination, Tom." The man should have known that. He'd served on the church board. "There isn't any 'they' to appoint us. We get called by the local church. Unless you throw me out, I could be here another fifty years."

"Good," Tom said. "And then we'll bury you out at Garden Oaks."

Laughter was followed by a long silence as the limousine crawled past a series of fast food places and then the John Deere dealership on the outskirts of town. Boundary Avenue angled steeply from the left. Soon the procession would be on the open road and the hearse would set a faster pace. In another hour, Andrews calculated, he would be back at the church. He could pick up the letter before walking over to the Ramsey's for the post-funeral refreshments. Not that there was any hurry. Chances were that when he opened the letter he would find himself looking into another grave. Glad tidings came by telephone these days. Black-bordered news came by mail.

Still, that first letter had opened up a measure of hope: *Dear Mr. Andrews, Dr. Charles Claybaugh has given us your name . . .*

Much later, Andrews was at the point of despair when another letter had arrived in the same kind of envelope. He braced himself for being told kindly that he had been eliminated. But Jim Purdy's note had taken him by surprise:

*Dear Jack:*
    *Just a line to let you know that we haven't forgotten*

*you. Our deliberations are taking a little longer than we anticipated. We expect to come to a decision in the next few days.*

That was nice of Jim. It looked as if the committee had deadlocked. Maybe they were still deadlocked and writing to ask a few more questions. Andrew would not give up hope until he opened the latest envelope. Not entirely.

From somewhere behind the limousine came a squeal of tires, then a series of crashing sounds. Andrews sensed a jolt of colliding vehicles. There were screams, shouts. The hearse in front of the limousine halted so abruptly the minister half expected the force of the stop to send the coffin hurtling through its windshield. To avoid smashing into the hearse, Old Greene pulled onto the shoulder and stopped. He turned off the engine, sighed heavily, and sat staring at the clock on the dashboard, as if the thing he always feared finally had caught up with him.

# CHAPTER TWO

A crowd was gathered where a small pickup truck had careened down the Boundary Avenue hill and into the second T. C. Greene & Son Cadillac. It was the same car that had taken Andrews from the parsonage to the funeral home. In the procession, it had been carrying members of the deceased's immediate family. None of them appeared to be hurt, although one or two sniffed the smelling salts that Old Greene, roused from momentary paralysis, administered to them. Andrews doubted that the funeral director ever went anywhere without his smelling salts, certainly not to any burial. Andrews himself had a small bottle of the pungent liquid in the top drawer of his bureau. It had been presented to him by Old Greene one day, along with the observation that one never knew when it might come in handy. So far, Andrews had found no occasion to use the bottle, and he doubted that he ever would. His wife Kate periodically complained that the bottle was in the way and asked him if she could throw it out. But he resisted. He told her that the bottle of smelling salts was the one bit of payola he had ever received and that he meant to keep it. He could not have articulated the true reason. Perhaps the daily discovery of the smelling salts among his socks and handkerchiefs lent to his life an edge of excitement, even urgency.

Greene & Son conferred about the Cadillac. The radiator was leaking. After the police had surveyed the scene, the car would have to be towed away. The deceased's family was all for finding places in other cars and proceeding immediately to the cemetery.

"They're expecting us back at the house in an hour," Myra Ramsey announced. "The refreshments are all ready."

But the first police to arrive wanted everyone in the car carried off to the hospital emergency room. None of the family would agree, least of all the Harper Wire and Cable executive, who kept urging, "Let's get this show back on the road."

As a compromise, it was agreed to let Dr. Otte look everyone over. The doctor, who was eighty-three, was riding in the last car of the procession. It took him a good ten minutes to reach the damaged Cadillac by foot, and another thirty to announce that everyone was in "tiptop shape, so far as I can tell." Fortunately, the young nurse who arrived with the volunteer ambulance crew was inclined to support his opinion.

There was also the driver of the pickup to consider. A high school boy, no more than seventeen, he had braked at the last second and tried to avoid collision by turning into a driveway. But he was going much too fast for this maneuver to succeed. His light truck flipped over and slid along its top into the funeral car, which in the same interval had swerved into the middle of the street. The sound of the crash was still ringing in everyone's ears when the boy popped out of the pickup like a circus clown.

"The light was green!" he shouted. "The light was green!"

The boy, too, denied any need for medical attention. But this time the police and the nurse were not convinced. He was laid out on a stretcher and placed into the ambulance. Andrews could hear the boy protesting as the volunteer paramedics drove him away.

The Harper Wire and Cable executive said to no one in particular, "Now can we get this show on the road?"

But the road was jammed. The immobilized Cadillac and the wrecked pickup effectively blocked the intersection. Traffic lined both avenues, including the cars in the St. Philomena procession, which were on their way to the Catholic cemetery at the other end of town. Greene & Son's two lead vehicles, the hearse and the limousine bearing the minister and pallbearers, were in the clear. But everyone else headed for Garden Oaks was stuck. Half of New Sharon's police force was now huddled under the traffic light, trying to work out a solution. Andrews wandered over to the boulder decorating the lawn of Peterson Appliance and sat down. He would be late getting back to the church today.

Andrews was also late coming home the day in August when the first letter arrived. He had gone into the city for the monthly clergy meeting and then stopped by to see Mrs. Homer at the state hospital. By the time he arrived at the church, Millie was gone—she only worked from one until four—and the mail addressed to him was stuck in his pigeonhole by the office door. He pulled out the whole pile—letters, advertisements, and three messages from Millie about the Sunday announcements—and took the bundle to the parsonage. He wanted to be home. The day was steaming and he was tired.

Kate started putting dinner on the table as soon as he walked through the door. "Do you have a meeting tonight?" she asked.

"No. That's one good thing about this time of year. Not many meetings."

"Thank God."

He brought the mail to the table and thumbed through it quickly. He recognized his prep school logo: Clover Hill Country Day abstracted to a circular blossom atop the crest of a triangular peak. Inside he would find a request for funds. He put the envelope aside, but later he would read the form letter carefully despite the fact that he could not afford to give. He always read these communications from Clover Hill even though he had not been particularly happy at that school and disapproved of its elitism. It was thirty years since he had seen any of his classmates. Still, it was a tie that bound. As the years passed, he found that his most ancient loyalties were the strongest.

His eye fixed on a piece of mail marked "Personal and Confidential." The thing had an ominous look. Something he had done wrong? Something he should not have said? Someone he had neglected? He did not want to deal with it at that moment; yet as Kate set the main course in front of him, he cut open the envelope with his dinner knife:

*Dear Mr. Andrews:*

*Dr. Charles Clayburgh of the district office has given us your name as someone who might be interested in the position of senior minister at Epiphany Church. As you may know, Dr. Norman Goodens, who served here for seventeen years, retired in April and . . .*

"It's not good manners," Kate said. The lines across her broad forehead were bent in a gentle censure.

Andrews looked up, not comprehending.

"Reading your mail at the dinner table. I don't see you all day, and now—"

"I'm sorry," he said, "it's just that I didn't have a chance to look at the mail, and this thing was marked personal."

"Another of your romantic intrigues?"

He smiled. "I hoped it might be, but it seems to be about a job."

The telephone rang. Over Kate's cry of protest, he

pushed back his chair and handed her the letter. "Here, you can take a look." He ran for the phone.

"Hello, Revner, this is Mabel Schatz."

"Oh, Mabel. How are you? I don't think I saw you Sunday."

"You didn't, Revner. We had to go to Kay's to watch the babies while they were looking into the septic tank."

"Looking into it?" He saw that Kate was bent over the letter, reading intently.

"They have a lot of problems out there," Mabel said, "living beyond the city services. Frank warned them more than once. He said, 'If you live beyond the services, you'll regret it.' But you can't tell young people anything, can you, Reverend Andrews?"

"Not very much."

"No, you can't tell young people anything today. How's Miriam, by the way?"

"Miriam? Oh, fine. She just got her Ph.D."

Kate was pointing to his plate where the pot roast was losing its steam.

"Isn't that something! Her Ph.D. It seems only yesterday you were so upset about her wanting to hitchhike to Alaska."

Turning his back on Kate, he gritted his teeth.

"I suppose I was upset," he said, "but I didn't think it showed."

"Oh, there's some of us can always tell those things, Jack."

He liked Mabel. Sometimes he thought she was his best

friend. But he wanted her to come to the point. Maybe silence would help.

In time he heard Mabel sigh. "Yes, indeedy. And now she's got her Ph.D. Now tell me why I called."

"You were saying something about your daughter's septic tank."

"Was I? That wasn't it." Mabel was breathing heavily as if searching through dense thickets of memory. At last she said, "It was the peas."

"Peas?"

"The peas, Revner, for the May church doings when we're entertaining all those folks from out of town. You see, Esther Circle was supposed to be in charge. It's their turn. But they couldn't get nobody to work. So as usual, Dorcas stepped in. Esther said they'd make some decorations, but, you know, Revner, it's a hardship on us when the younger women don't want to work."

"They have a lot of other things to do," he said. "Most of them have jobs."

"I know." Mabel sighed again. "It's a shame. Life is becoming too materialistic, don't you think?"

"I can't deny that, Mabel, but some of those young women need to work to support their families. And others want to make the best use of their talents. Just staying home and vacuuming the floor isn't all that fulfilling."

He would have liked to see the expression on Kate's face. He was tempted to turn around, but he dared not look at her.

Mabel was saying that she used to think helping with the

Christmas Bazaar was the most fulfilling event of the year. "Life is more than soft raiment," she concluded.

"I guess so, Mabel. But what's this about peas?"

"The opinion's been expressed at the Dorcas board that men don't like peas. What do you think about that?"

"Well, I think most men like peas. Some, I suppose, do not. I didn't know it was a question of sex."

"It's not that we want to bring sex into it, Revner. We wouldn't want anything like that. I always thought peas were safe that way. It's just that some of the ladies believe the men don't like them. I told the board, 'Frank likes peas and so do our two boys.' Oh, maybe when they were little tykes they balked some. Jimmie would have nothing to do with cooked carrots when he was six years old. He spit them right out once at the table and Frank was about to take a strap to him he was so mad. But Jimmie eats carrots well enough now and peas, too—"

"I'm glad your boys like peas, Mabel, but what's the alternative?"

"What's that, Revner?"

"What could the Dorcas serve instead of peas?"

"That's just it." She was nearly breathless, her words coming faster and faster. "What could we serve? We were all settled on peas and then somebody said, 'Give them string beans.' Now aside from their being expensive that time of the year, coming all the way from Peru or wherever, you have to cut beans up. And do you think Esther Circle is about to help with that? And some people can't eat beans. They catch in their throats. Who's to say that Dr. Smythe

21

would be there, seeing he's always getting calls on that little radio he carries around—"

He cut her off again. "I see you have a problem," he told her, "but peas or beans, I don't think it's that big an issue."

"It's the principle of the thing, Revner."

"It always is." He turned toward Kate again and grinned. She did not grin back.

"When people decide something they ought to stick to it," Mabel said.

"Like getting married and paying their church pledge."

"You're so right, Reverend Andrews. Also, you don't change the menu at a meeting called to discuss table cloths."

Kate picked up his plate and disappeared into the kitchen.

Mabel was asking, "Can I quote you, Revner, at the executive committee meeting?"

"Quote me?"

"As to your liking peas."

"Oh, sure."

"And I promise not to bring sex into it, because I know you don't want anything like that in church."

"Certainly not."

"Well, I won't take any more of your time, Revner. I know the burdens you carry every day. When people say they wonder what you do all week, I tell them they'd be surprised at some of the things you get into."

"Yes, I think they would."

"Yes, indeed! All right then, Revner. Remember me to

Kate and tell her I'm so glad Miriam gave up that business about climbing Mount McKinley."

She hung up before he could reply. As he resumed his seat at the table, Kate reappeared with his plate. She had been warming it in the microwave. "That was Mabel Schatz," he told her.

"You don't say."

He began to eat. Kate had put on her glasses and was poring over the letter again. He smiled at her frown of concentration. He could imagine her looking just like that peering down a list of words for a spelling lesson in the fourth grade.

"It's not that serious," he said. "They've repealed the draft law."

"This is wonderful. It's a university church. And you'd be senior minister with multiple staff."

"Somebody will be. Not likely myself."

He saw her color rise. "But you will write, Jack, to say you're interested. It's just the sort of place you've always wanted. It would be so stimulating for you."

He grunted. "I think I'm past stimulating."

"Jack, it's just what you've always wanted. A university town, an active adult-education program, a social-concerns ministry. And a modern plant, by the sound of it. Did you see the fact sheet they sent along?"

"I haven't had a chance yet. But if there's one thing I've learned in seeking the proverbial larger field of service, it is that you can't trust most of the facts supplied by pastoral search committees."

Kate clamped her lips together, took off her glasses, and went into the kitchen. Andrews reached for the letter and the accompanying fact sheet. He read them quickly, then looked up and pondered his reflection in the door of the china closet. His bleached image merged with the white cups and saucers.

When Kate came back with two dishes of tapioca pudding, she said, "I really think that this Epiphany Church is the best thing you've heard from."

Her enthusiasm irritated him. "I wouldn't make too much of it," he told her. "Of the twenty or so people that letter went to, at least nineteen are likely to be younger than I."

Then he was angry with himself. He wanted her to be excited about the letter, and he wanted her to be encouraging. But he didn't want her to expect anything. He knew she would want his opinion of the pudding, so he rolled the first spoonful around in his mouth judiciously. He told her that it was just right, not at all soupy.

"I tried putting it in the refrigerator right away this time," Kate said. "It seems to thicken better that way." She took a spoonful herself and, looking satisfied, added, "You know, Jack, I don't think you should be so self-conscious about your age. I think people are looking for more maturity in positions of leadership these days. So you're fifty-eight. Some presidents of the United States have been a lot older than that."

"That's true, but what churches want is a father figure of thirty-nine."

"You sound as if you were ready for the county home,

when the truth is you're just at the height of your powers."

"Possibly. I'm just reflecting the way pulpit committees look at things. Let's face it, I've had my name in circulation for over two years."

It was true. A dozen or more letters like this one had come. One even led to an interview. It was with a church in one of the newer suburbs of Milwaukee. A member of the search committee kept driving him by all the schools in the neighborhood until he got through to her that his children were grown. That, he sensed, was more of a barrier than his actual age. He could not offer a parsonage family that fit the community's self-image. He had seen the church photo directory, which revealed that the congregation had changed considerably since the days of its baby boom origins. It was evident that couples with children under twenty were now a minority of the membership. But the committee did not see the church that way, or if it did, it clung to the belief that a minister with young children would lead them back to their heroic era.

Kate was watching him. "But you will answer. You will look into it."

"I'll think about it."

"Please, Jack." She reached across the table and touched his hand.

He took his hand away, walked into the living room, and sat in his favorite chair. He always thought the one graceful feature about the parsonage was the archway that led to the small dining room. Kate was standing under it. She looked very small there, as if diminished by stretches of classical time and space.

"Why not answer them right away? This evening, since you don't have to go out. Send them your best enthusiastic response. After all, what have you got to lose?"

"Possibly my pride."

"Isn't that the ultimate sin?"

"So they say, which may be why I hoard the little I have left. A man can only take so many rejections."

She turned away and began clearing the table. She moved out of sight, but he could see her shadow against the wall, bending over. Suddenly remorseful, he left his chair and followed her into the kitchen, taking with him his dessert dish.

"I don't know why I got started trying to move," he said. "I have a good church now. With the decline that's set in among the liberal denominations, most of my colleagues would consider this a prize. We have a larger than average membership, a reasonably supportive congregation that is used to me. And I'm used to them. It's not a bad town. I really don't think either one of us would care anymore for an urban environment. Aside from a last gasp of ambition, there's no compelling reason why I shouldn't stay here until I retire."

She put the dishes she was carrying down on the counter beside the sink, turned slowly, and looked at him. "You're the one who always says that a minister shouldn't stay in a church more than ten years."

"I know. That's one of the many stupid things they taught me in seminary." He began helping her put things into the dishwasher. Just a year old, and installed with great parochial fanfare, the washer was the parsonage's latest concession to modernity. "The truth is," he said, "I'm comfortable here. You're comfortable, too."

"Maybe that's what's wrong with us," she said.

He watched her until she had all the dishes in place and had set the wash cycle in motion. "You really don't want to move again," he said quietly. "I know this is not your ideal existence, but I think you've grown to like it some. You could teach full time now if you wanted to. In fact, Mr. Waycross at the high school asked me the other day if you'd be interested. I saw him at Rotary. I think people would accept your working now. You'd be surprised."

Her back was to him again. "I don't want to teach full time. That has nothing to do with it."

"But I can't believe you'd be so anxious for me to seek a call elsewhere if you had only yourself to consider."

She faced him. "But there isn't only myself, you see. You're withering away here and so am I."

He laughed and went back to the living room.

Ten minutes later, Kate stood under the arch, looming larger than before. She still had that Vassar posture.

"So what are you going to do, Jack?"

"I'm going to answer that letter saying I am enraptured by the opportunity to be considered for the opening. I'll write my answer this evening and take the letter down to the box outside the post office so that it goes out at six a.m. Only first, I have something else in mind."

"Oh, what's that?"

"To show you that I am not withering away in every respect. I am going to take you upstairs and remove your intimate apparel."

# CHAPTER THREE

"Oh, Reverend. Reverend Andrews." Someone standing by the fire hydrant was calling his name. "Reverend Andrews, if you'll come back to the car, we'll be starting for the cemetery."

Andrews rose from his seat on the boulder and looked around. The scene hadn't changed much. The pickup was still in the same place and still overturned. The disabled funeral car was still there, too, though a tow truck had taken a position in front of it. But there seemed to be some movement up the Boundary Avenue hill. He arrived at the pallbearers' car the same time as Tom Crossman, the man from his church.

"Old Greene says we're about to start," Tom said, "though I can't see what the point is. Everyone else is still tied up."

"We'll see," Andrews said, and climbed into the car. It always amused him to hear the funeral director called by that name. Of course, no one ever called him "Old Greene" to his face.

"What's up, Ted?" It was the sepulchral voice again.

Andrews turned to look as the figure stopped to enter the rear door of the limousine. He was a man of about sixty, tall and thin, with a long, pock-marked face. He fit the type Andrews once read about as having an extra Y chromosome, a type said to be inclined to violence. But such a man could hardly be on a first-name basis with Old Greene.

"We'll be going on," Old Greene said. "Us and the hearse. I'd just as soon get there a little ahead of the others, anyway, so's to make sure things are right at the grave. You never can be sure what they'll do at these country cemeteries. Course, the flower car must be nearly out there by now, but I like to make sure about things myself."

"But what about the rest of the procession?" someone asked.

"They'll have to back up and take Elmwood Avenue to Peterson Road and then out to the highway from there."

"That's going to take a while."

"Yep."

They were all inside now waiting for Young Greene to start the hearse. The man who believed Reverend Cruller was still at his church had suddenly remembered he had a three-thirty appointment. "Jesus! Pardon my language, Reverend, but what am I going to do?"

It was one of the many questions put to Andrews these days that he did not presume to answer.

They were out on the highway again, the hearse setting a pace of fifty miles per hour. The conversation continued, subdued but unceasing. Once in a while the voices directed a question to the funeral director, but they left the minister alone. Perhaps they sensed that he was not in the mood for small talk. He was marking a large occasion.

Andrews enjoyed looking at the countryside. It was rolling farmland, open fields except for small stands of oak and maple atop the larger hills. Some of the grain fields were newly ploughed after harvesting. Others lay fallow. Most of the corn was gone, but some frayed stalks were still standing. Every half mile a cluster of silos rose above a square white house and one or more red barns. Usually the house was shielded to the west and north by a cluster of dark spruce. There were cattle on the hillsides—with rare exceptions, angular Holsteins. While some bright orange pumpkins still lay in the fields, others had been gathered in piles on front lawns, lined up between the turned pillars of Victorian porches. Occasionally, a small apple orchard appeared near a house, the trees still freighted with red fruit. A line of verse came to Andrews, something he had memorized for an exam for a course in the English Romantics: "To bend with apples the moss'd cottage-trees."

No moss that he could see, but the feeling was right, except that the season was more advanced than in Keats's tribute to ripeness. It was a ripeness on the far edge.

*Then in a wailful choir the small gnats mourn.*

He must have memorized the whole thing. Not that he could recite much more of it now. The scattered lines took him by surprise. It had been a dull course, everything classified into categories that had little to do with the poetry itself. And he had rebelled at the memorization, though, in the end, he begged a benzedrine tablet from a classmate whose father was a doctor, and stayed up all night to memorize three hundred lines. During the morning exam, his mind suddenly had gone blank. He doubted he could have told anyone his name. Somehow he managed a C+ on the test. But now these lines came back to him as an extra credit, something gratis, *gratia plena*, like the pumpkins and the crimson sumac along the railroad tracks.

Ahead, a yellow school bus flashed its red warning. The hearse slowed to a stop, and behind it, the limousine. Two children, a large girl and a small boy, jumped off the bus and ran across the road toward a low ranch house. As the boy darted ahead, the girl stopped at the aluminum mailbox held up by the pink fist of a wooden Uncle Sam. Andrews had noticed this before: the first thing many children did on leaving the school bus was to head for the mailbox. It was a sign of modern times, that their mothers were not home. But it was no less a sign to him that, even for the coming generation, promises lurked within the printed envelope.

*Dr. Clayburgh has given us your name.*

The limousine was nearing Clove Road and would be turning right. He could always tell that corner by the pair of tall pines that became visible as soon as he crossed the little bridge some two miles away. The trees reminded him of those in the old Hamm's Beer ads, quirky evergreens behind a grinning bear. No Christmas card perfection, these trees had the irregularity of form characteristic of white pines as they grow older. More than once the thought had occurred to him that aging white pines were like people. When he was very young, it seemed to him that old people were all alike. He had trouble telling them apart. But as he grew older himself, he learned that the sameness was superficial. Though they might look alike, the senior members of his congregation were far more distinctive than the younger ones in mind and spirit. Quirkier. He knew that, when he left New Sharon, it would be the old people he would remember most.

The funeral car slowed as it neared the pines, which partially obscured a house on the corner. It was a small house with dormers upstairs (they would call it a "cape" back East), painted a shade of light blue that reminded Andrews of a set of dominoes he had owned as a child. The dots were that same color, bright enough, he had imagined, to glow in the dark. They hadn't, though; he had tested his hypothesis in his closet with the door closed.

Old Greene eased the Cadillac gently around the corner and, in the passing, Andrews thought of the pale blue dominoes once again.

Ahead, the hearse proceeded cautiously. In contrast to the highway, which had been coated with asphalt the previous spring, Clove Road was full of potholes that had widened and deepened over many winters.

"Not nice to jiggle the dead that way," Tom called from the backseat. He broke into giggles.

"Can't help it," Old Greene said. "This road's like the surface of the moon."

"Going over it's enough to wake the dead," Tom said and giggled again.

"I hope not," Andrews quipped, "otherwise we've come all this way for nothing." Startled by his own irreverence, he shrank down in the upholstered seat.

But everyone laughed, even Old Greene.

The sepulchral voice said: "Say, Ted, did you handle the Klinger funeral?"

Old Greene kept his eyes fixed on the potholes. "No, Kappelmeister had the Klinger funeral. He was Lutheran, you know. Missouri Synod."

"No, I didn't know that."

"Well, it was really more his wife. We get quite a few of the Lutherans, most everything, in fact. But Kappelmeister sort of specialized in the Missouri Synod folk." For an instant, Old Greene took his eyes off the road and turned to Andrews. "You ever work with Kappelmeister, Reverend?"

"Now and then. I've had a few with Donegan."

Old Greene nodded, his eyes front again. It was taken for granted that, at the appropriate time, most of the people in Andrews' congregation would turn to T. C. Greene & Son. The same was true of the Methodists and the Episcopalians. Increasingly, the more liberal Lutherans, and even some of the Catholics, sought out the services of Greene. But the choice of funeral director was often a matter of family tradition, persisting through changes in church affiliation. Some people even called in Harris & Tofte from Hawk Rapids, twenty miles away. About three deaths out of four, though, Andrews worked with Greene.

Carrie Campbell was one of the exceptions. She had left directions with her daughter that she wanted to be cremated. The Campbells were among the oldest and wealthiest families in New Sharon. The family had always turned to T. C. Greene & Son in the past, and had always had their deceased embalmed and buried. So when Angela Campbell telephoned and asked one of the Greene assistants about cremation, she received a curt response. Angela then called Donegan, setting off a quake in the mortuarial universe.

"Why didn't Miss Campbell identify herself on the phone?" Young Greene had asked Andrews.

"I can't say," Andrews told him. "She didn't consult with me." But he had suspected that Angela wanted a response unbiased by her social position. And she got it. The Catholic undertaker cheerfully arranging for the cremation was an added irony that Angela obviously had relished.

The funeral car idled before the cemetery gate. Garden Oaks was an old cemetery that rose on a hillside just before the road descended into the hamlet of Clove Valley. Among the two hundred or so grave markers, the same family names repeated—Locksley, Allendorfer, Baird, Cummage. All were familiar names to Andrews. He never came to Garden Oaks without being reminded that a large portion of his congregation shared these rural origins. Not that the place where he lived and served was a metropolis. The population of New Sharon had reached ten thousand in the last census, but it was said that, in order to arrive at this number, the census takers had counted the dead in the Catholic cemetery, which lay within the municipal borders. Another story making the rounds of New Sharon's twenty-three taverns was that the census had also included cows from a nearby dairy farm. The increase of two hundred people since the previous census had come as a surprise, especially since both the cannery and the milking machine factory had closed during the last decade. There were those who believed that the Chamber of Commerce had connived with Congressman Peterson to have the figure rounded upward.

Even at an honest ten thousand, New Sharon was a small town. Still, it was the largest for some miles around and had the distinction of serving as the county seat. People who lived there saw themselves in a different light from the citizens of Clove Valley, or even Kane City, the home of twenty-five hundred souls, located five miles south on Highway 303. The spirit with which the New Sharon Rotarians greeted the club from Kane City at their annual joint meeting was always marked by a special quality of cordial condescension.

As the silver hearse led the matching limousine slowly under the wrought iron archway with the legend GARDEN OAKS and down a rutted drive, Andrews could see that a tent had been set up over the grave. Some distance beyond the tent the flower car was parked.

"I thought the other cars might have beat us here," Frank said. "I figured that going up Peterson to the highway, they could take that back way in here."

"I hope they didn't," Old Greene said. "If you think Clove Road is bad, you ought to see that one. I doubt they could get down it at all." He swung the big car onto a narrow strip of turf between the rutted drive and a row of grave markers. "I think I'll just go on by a little," he told them, "so's the other cars can come in close." He pulled back onto the drive and stopped just ahead of the hearse.

It was Old Greene's one departure from the beaten path, Andrews told himself—the habit of driving on grass. One spring Greene had cut across a low area in the big cemetery just outside of town and gotten stuck. Andrews and the pallbearers had to walk through muck to reach the grave.

Old Greene turned off the ignition. "Might be a good idea, boys," he said, "to take a stretch."

As the pallbearers climbed slowly out of the recesses of the limousine, the driver of the flower car walked over from where he was sitting against a tree. Unlike the other Greene men, he was dressed in work clothes.

"What the hell happened?" he asked.

"Accident at the Boundary Avenue light," a pallbearer told him. "We're lucky to be alive."

The flower car driver stared at the limousine. "You don't look like you've been hit."

"It was the car behind us, the family car," Old Greene explained. "Crazy kid came down the hill."

"Should have been a cop there," Frank said.

Old Greene shrugged. "Anyway," he said to the flower car driver, "nobody was hurt, except maybe the kid a little.

But the rest of the procession's got to come out of town another way."

"When do you think they'll get here?" the driver asked.

"Can't say. Could be a while yet," Old Greene answered.

"Damn!" Frank said very loudly. "And I've got to be somewhere at three." He pulled out a pack of cigarettes, walked over to a stone bench, and sat down.

Andrews decided to follow Old Greene's advice to stretch his legs. He started up a gravel path toward a clump of pyramidal arbor vitae. Tom fell in beside him.

"Makes you think, doesn't it, Reverend, an accident like that."

"How's that?"

"Well, a few feet difference, and it could have been our car. And maybe a slightly different angle, and somebody could have been killed. One of us, maybe. Makes you think."

"Yes, it does," Andrews said. It was the first sign that any of them had been shaken by the incident. He hadn't reacted to it much himself—probably too distracted.

"Prepare to meet thy God. Right, Reverend?"

"Right, Tom. You never know."

The path was growing quite steep, and Tom was a short heavy man with an asthmatic wheeze. He stopped abruptly. "Well, Reverend, I think I'll leave you to go on alone." He turned back toward the car.

Andrews went by an even narrower path to the top of the hill where a granite obelisk stood. He was curious to see what name it bore. After brushing away the obscuring dirt, he found that the monument read "Watkins" on one side, "Moore" on the other. A cooperative venture prompted, no doubt, by a marriage between the two families. The small markers scattered about might have told him more, had he the desire to examine them. But he preferred to gaze out over the valley. He recalled someone telling him that Garden Oaks Cemetery contained the highest point in the county. The Moores, he noted, faced the stand of arbor vitae. The Watkinses took the long view.

He saw that the last of the pallbearers had huddled around the limousine. Young Greene had left the hearse and was looking down into the grave, accompanied by a man in overalls who had emerged from the farmhouse just beyond the lower wall. Andrews had seen the man, the sexton at Garden Oaks, before. A carpet of unnatural green had been spread around the grave. Young Greene and the farmer/sexton knelt down to pull the carpet smooth while the flower car driver banked one side of the grave with chrysanthemums and gladioli. Out on Clove Road there was no sign of an approaching procession.

The minister searched to find where the main highway appeared from behind a broad, low hill. In England it might have been called a "down." He and Kate had gone to England once, for the three-month sabbatical the church had granted him after eight years of service. It was the recent policy of his denomination to promote sabbaticals, and, while the notion was new to his church officers, they agreed to the idea as long as he paid his own way and took his leave during the summer. He hadn't pursued a formal study program. But he and Kate had visited a variety of ecclesiastical establishments. When they returned, everyone was pleased with their colored slides of cathedrals.

Andrews noticed that a telephone company vehicle was parked along the visible stretch of highway. He could just make out a man high on a pole. Another man stood below. A sudden gush of envy rose in Andrews. To possess so definable and serviceable a skill. To set down your empty lunchbox on an evening, knowing you had fixed this and installed that. To go out to meet emergencies in the face of wind and hail, failing perhaps, falling even, yet in a clear and measurable line of duty. To be indispensable to the message, someone without whose good offices even the Word might fail.

Andrews himself was never at ease on a telephone line. With the changes in models, he was never certain which end of the phone was which. And when he found the correct end, he often was smitten by a kind of aphasia. He rarely said anything important by phone. If there was something important to say, or to listen to, he preferred either to write or to converse in person. He could not reach out and touch by telephone. Consequently, he was, at times, out of touch. It was one of an increasing number of ways, he feared, in which the world and he were communicating at a long distance over a bad connection.

Telephone calls often took Andrews by surprise. He had been taking a little nap that evening in the summer when the phone rang in the tiny downstairs bedroom he used as a den.

Ten days of silence had followed his reply by mail to the Epiphany search committee. Knowing how slowly such committees worked, especially during summer, he was not discouraged by the lapse of time. Then by express mail, he received a large folder containing the church's official "profile," together with various items prepared by the local Chamber of Commerce. The profile offered facts and figures about the church and the results of a membership survey concerning the congregation's needs and interests, as well as the qualities sought in a new senior pastor. Andrews had glanced at the folder quickly when it arrived at the church office. Then he had taken it to the parsonage. He hadn't wanted Millie or anyone else to catch a glimpse of it and get ideas. Fortunately, the folder was right at his elbow when the ringing phone jerked him from the early stages of sleep into a violent startle response.

"Hello. Dr. Andrews?"

"Yes." He hadn't earned that title, but until he knew who was calling there was no point quibbling.

"Dr. Andrews, this is Jim Purdy of Epiphany Church. How is it out there—wet and blustery like it is here?"

"Just damp and overcast." He reached for the comb that he kept in his desk drawer and pulled it through his hair.

"I was hoping you would say the sun was out. Most of our weather comes from your way." The voice modulated into a more enterprising tone. "Dr. Andrews, did you receive the packet of materials we sent?"

"Yes, I did. It just arrived yesterday."

"How did it impress you?"

Andrews cleared his throat. "It impressed me very favorably. By that I mean, not only is the church itself impressive in its program, but your committee did an excellent job in presenting the facts." He was opening the folder with his free hand. "I especially like the succinct way it sums up the major trends in the life of the church over the last ten years under various headings."

The truth was that it was a better profile than most. Later, if things went further, he would ask for other documents. But as church profiles went, it was informative. And in its frank witness to an aging and declining membership, it certainly was no snow job.

"I know the committee will be glad to hear of your reaction," Purdy said. "They spent more than three months working on it. Too much time in my opinion. But then I'm the businessman on the committee, and I like to get things done."

Andrews decided by the sound of the voice that Jim Purdy was an older man. His was a pleasant voice, warm and down to earth, but shrewd, too. Andrews asked what kind of business Purdy was in and was told that he ran a real estate and insurance agency.

"They put me on the committee to keep the academic types in line. Now, Dr. Andrews, might you be interested in looking further into our pastorate?"

"I believe so." He would not sound too eager. Nor indifferent either. "Yes, very much so."

"Good. I'm glad to hear you say that. Now if you've no objection, we'd like to send a small delegation to attend one of your Sunday services sometime soon."

"That would be fine."

"How about Sunday the fifteenth?"

"That sounds good. Let me check my calendar." He knew there was no need, but he fingered through the pocket-sized date book he kept with him at all times. "The fifteenth would be fine, Mr. Purdy."

"Good. And you'll be preaching that day?"

"Oh yes." He thought, who else?

"Fine. Well, Dr. Andrews, I'll be in touch in a few days as to who exactly will be coming. We're arranging several of these visits, you see."

So they still had several candidates in view. Purdy was letting him know.

"I'll be looking forward to it, Mr. Purdy. I should tell you, though, that you've been doing me an honor I don't deserve. I don't have a doctorate, honorary or otherwise."

Purdy's chuckle was reassuring. "I'm almost glad to hear it. We've got so many doctors of one sort or another around this church. Do you mind if I call you John?"

What name he went by depended on the setting. He always had been John at home. But "Jack" fit in with the air of informality that people looked for in a minister these days. A questionnaire used by the denomination asked parishioners if their minister was "formal" or "informal." It was like asking if he were sinister or affable.

He always thought of himself as Andrews. That was how he'd been known since he began attending Clover Hill Country Day in the sixth grade. It was a boy's school, and everyone was called by his last name, both by students and teachers. The same was true of the boarding school he went to later on. Sometimes the boys might call a close friend by his first name, or more likely by a nickname derived from his last name—like "Tred," for instance, the name he had called his best friend Carter Treadwell, who was now president of Logan and Associates, a money management firm. But Andrews was always Andrews to Tred and even to George Hayes, whom he had known from this earliest Clover Hill days. Only a few weeks ago, Andrews had received a letter out of the blue from George, asking for a loan. It began: "Dear Andrews . . ."

Andrews said to Purdy: "I'd be happy to have you call me John, but I usually go by Jack these days."

"Okay, Jack, and I'm Jim."

Now as he looked out over the valley, something strange was happening just beyond the telephone truck, at a place where the highway was joined by a narrow dirt road. It was the back road to the cemetery that Old Greene had pronounced impassable. One by one a long string of cars was turning onto the road. The cars had their lights on. Andrews walked quickly down the hill to report the news. In advance, he granted a plenary indulgence for any and all expletives that might inadvertently reach his ears.

# CHAPTER FOUR

Theoretically, Young Greene was in charge these days, his father performing only a backup and advisory role. And in practice, Old Greene was spending less time around the mortuary. He let his son handle most of the smaller funerals. But when old families were involved, Old Greene was certain to be on the scene, and when he was there it was taken for granted by everyone that he had the last word. For a man such as Old Greene, it was hard to yield position and place, especially when so many others conspired to keep him where he had always been. Still, he was a man bred to long perspectives; he knew that the day was approaching when Young Greene would become Old Greene, and increasingly he stepped aside and let his son take the lead at each decisive turn in the typical afternoon's proceedings. He stood aside, now, as Young Greene supervised the brief passage of the casket from the hearse to the grave. Positioned just outside the tent, Old Greene might have been taken from a distance as a tall monument of black marble, looming above the gray granite headstones.

Old Greene kept everything and everyone in view. He was pleased the family had chosen a top-of-the-line mahogany casket. It was a shame the way the flag covered so much of it. He hoped young Ted would see that the flag was smoothed out properly when the pallbearers set the casket down. He liked the way Reverend Andrews' interment services were short and to the point. He remembered the time about nine years ago in January when he and Andrews went out together to Oak Hill to bury that old fellow found dead in a little shack on Forest Street. The man had lain by a gas heater for three days. Nothing they did stopped the odor entirely; just as well that it was twenty below outside. The old fellow's was a county burial, and the only people to help carry the casket were the cemetery man and Reverend Andrews, who didn't hesitate at all to take one side.

"I don't want to tell you what to do, Reverend," Old Greene had said to the minister, "but considering everything, I think I'd just say, 'I commit you to the ground,' and be done with it."

Reverend Andrews had spoken a few more words than that, but not many.

Andrews was all right once you got used to him, but some of these younger ministers were a problem. That woman at the Center Valley Church was typical of what Old Greene had to deal with these days. She wouldn't do a service, even in the funeral home, unless the casket was closed. Several times she got everybody upset. He knew of two families that had left her church over her behavior. She also made a fuss over the little prayer cards Greene & Son had for people during the viewing. She claimed the language wasn't "inclusive." Sure, Jack had his own sticky points. But he had been around quite awhile, and he knew how things should be done in New Sharon. God willing, he would stay on awhile longer.

The wind was rising again, a sharp, icy blast out of the northwest, and nothing on the hillside broke its force. Andrews dispelled for good any doubts he might have entertained about the wisdom of wearing his winter coat. It was still October. The fiery maples along the cemetery wall gave an illusion of warmth. But this was the upper Midwest—stress the "upper"—and it might snow tomorrow.

Andrews had taken his station at the head of the grave, and he was waiting. The family was in place, seated together in a row of chairs under the tent. The men from the Legion were lining up. But mourners from the most distant cars moved toward Andrews with a strange deliberation, as if they were picking their way through a mine field.

His eyes met those of Myra Ramsey. She was the only one of the family whom he really knew. A thin, twitchy woman, she was often around the church. For years she had been trying to get her father out of the sagging white house on Box Elder Street. She would corner Andrews during the coffee hour following the Sunday service and tell him how her father had slipped on the steps, or left the stove on overnight. But the old man resisted all attempts to get him into a retirement facility. Just two months earlier a stroke had sent him to the hospital and then to a nursing home.

Andrews looked down at the coffin, draped with an American flag. Only once had he called at the house. Mr. Upsall resented being thought of as a shut-in. Though he was friendly enough the few times he came to church, Upsall's response to the minister's telephone calls was always a curt "No need to check up on me, Pastor, I'm doing fine."

Once, Andrews dropped by with a plant that the women's group had sent in honor of Mr. Upsall's birthday. The women were going to have the florist deliver the plant directly, but Andrews grasped the opportunity to see the old man. The Upsall home was one of those houses built early in this century that looked like a perfect cube with various appendages tacked on: a big porch, two bay windows, and high dormers sticking out on all sides. There were two old rocking chairs on the porch, one of which, on this occasion, had a fat orange cat in it. The cat blinked as Andrews went up the steps, but otherwise registered no interest in his appearance. Andrews could hear the shrill bell ringing when he pushed the button, then a series of movements somewhere deep inside the house. He wondered how the old man would react.

To his relief, Mr. Upsall was glad to see him. The old man received the plant with obvious pleasure and led Andrews into a front room full of heavy objects and complex odors. Curtains of Quaker lace reduced the sun to a wraith on that brilliant summer day. In the center of the room was a long, narrow table covered with a cloth of greenish gold. On the table, a large scrapbook lay open. The old man took the plant and set it next to the book.

"I'll leave it there for now, Reverend, until I figure out where to keep it. What is it, a begonia?"

"I think so. It probably would be best to put it where it can get some sunlight."

The old man nodded. "I guess so. I'll probably put it in the kitchen window where the morning sun comes in. I spend a lot of time there most mornings." He contemplated the plant for a moment. "Nice color."

"Yes, it is," Andrews agreed. "A real fire engine red."

Mr. Upsall chuckled. "Yep. Brightens things up." He pointed to the scrapbook. "I was looking at that when you rang the bell."

The cutouts, Andrews noted, were of soldiers, mostly Scots Guards by the look of them.

"That's what we did for amusement in the old days, Pastor. No TV. No roller skating rinks." The old man's head, a narrow wedge of white and pink, hung at an angle over the table. It shook with a fine tremor.

"You grew up on a farm?"

The old man nodded. "Out on Cedar Creek, near to Clove Valley. That's where they'll bury me, you know—

Garden Oaks Cemetery." He looked at Andrews sharply as if to make sure this fact had registered. "When I was fifteen, my father sent me to board in town so I could go to the high school. Then I went into men's furnishings."

"Your daughter told me you had a shoe store."

"That came later. A lot later. When I came home from the war—that's World War I."

"Right."

"I bet you don't meet many people these days been in that war."

"No, I don't."

"No, they're mostly gone. Sit down, Reverend."

Andrews found a seat in a brown plush chair facing the piano. Mr. Upsall settled slowly into a black leather chair near the window.

"Well, as I was saying, after the war, I went to work for the Hub Men's Shop. That was on Main at the corner of Second in those days. I think there's a cafe there now, ain't there?"

Andrew tried to visualize that corner. Something was there. "It may be a cafe," he said.

"Well, anyway, I was there for twenty years. I'd saved up something in that time. So when I had the chance, I took over Maston's Shoes. The son—that's Jim Maston, maybe you knew him—didn't want the business. So I bought him out."

"Nice to have your own business."

"That's right." Mr. Upsall's eyes looked into the distance. "I got to join the Kiwanis then. But it was never much of a business. If the farm hadn't come to me, I wouldn't have had much. It was selling the farm got us this house." His pale blue eyes panned the room, taking possession one more time. "When I leave here, I'll be going out feet first. No other way."

The quavery voice fell silent. The old man seemed suddenly to have run out of words.

Andrews looked around. On the piano there was a large silver-framed photograph of a middle-aged woman. Andrews had never known Mrs. Upsall. She had died before he came to New Sharon.

"That's a nice picture on the piano," he said. "Is she your wife?"

"Yep."

Mr. Upsall sat looking at the photograph for a long while. But he volunteered nothing more, and Andrews sensed that this was not the time to try to draw him out. Instead, he rose to leave. The old man showed him to the door.

"Thank the ladies for the begonia, Reverend."

"I will."

The orange cat winked as Andrews went down the porch steps.

The last of the stragglers drew up behind the crowd huddled inside the tent. Young Greene stepped to the edge of the canopy and looked toward Andrews with just the barest hint of a nod. The minister took his service book out of his overcoat pocket. His committal services were generally straight from the book. His denomination did not require that, but he felt the service carried more authority, more universality as written. The traditional prayers with the biblical cadences put the event in the context of the ages. A funeral was no time for clerical showboating.

". . . and give you peace, Amen." Andrews closed his book.

Taps sounded. A very loud trumpet blast before the key was found, followed by ragged rifle fire. Then the flag was folded with tender care by a man whose uniform no longer fit. When he was finished, he presented the flag to Mrs. Ramsey, who looked up quickly, as if surprised, and let the bright cloth lie limply in her lap.

Andrews moved down the row of chairs, shaking hands with the immediate family: Mrs. Ramsey, her husband, and her brother from Harper Wire and Cable. He said a word or two to a young woman who stood just behind the Mrs. Ramsey and was crying. Then he left them to themselves and moved outside the tent. Once again, he had presumed to do something in the presence of that about which nothing could be done.

Alone again, he stood for a moment looking over the valley to where he knew Cedar Creek ran between the willows. Heavy clouds were beginning to move in, and the sky was darkening histrionically. Old-home week at the grave would not last long today. He walked briskly to the limousine.

Young Greene trailed behind him, "Could you use a couple of those sprays at the church, Reverend Andrews?"

He really couldn't. Memorial flowers for the altar had been scheduled months earlier. The funeral sprays would be wilted by Sunday morning, even the mums. But the family might like to have some of their flowers in the church and to have them mentioned from the pulpit. "You might have your man drop one of the sprays off at the church," Andrews said. "I don't think we can handle more than that."

"Okay, Reverend."

Young Greene started to leave, then turned back. "It was nice of you to come to the visitation," he said.

Andrews rarely went to visitations, but this time he had gone and sat with the family for a while. He wasn't sure why, except that, given Mr. Upsall's age, he didn't think many people would show up. He told Young Greene, "I just dropped in briefly. Mrs. Ramsey's sort of nervous, and her father was a nice old gentleman."

"Well, I'm glad you came by, Reverend." He paused, then added, "I thought Mr. Upsall looked real good, didn't you? I mean considering his age and the stroke and everything."

Andrews hadn't thought about it. He rarely gave an open coffin more than a passing glance. "Yes," he said. Every man needed commendation for his craft. "He looked fine."

The undertaker appeared pleased. "Okay, Reverend Andrews. Dad'll be here in a couple of minutes to drive you home."

Young Greene went back to confer with the family. Small knots of mourners gathered along the slope. The man who drove the flower car stood patiently to one side, talking to the grave digger. They would wait until all the mourners had left before lowering the coffin into the grave. Andrews, too, was waiting. He had brought the letter along, he might be reading it now without any sense of impropriety. His work was done.

# CHAPTER FIVE

Alone in the limousine, Andrews let his mind drift back. After Jim Purdy's call, another letter . . . Hilda Cox and Harry Bauman would be flying to Madison, staying over night, and coming to New Sharon in the morning by rented car. They understood the service time to be ten-thirty. But Andrews should please phone if there was a change in time. The note was dated September 3, and signed by Susan Grant, Secretary, Epiphany Church Pastoral Search Committee.

Andrews had expected a larger delegation. Yet, as he thought about it, he realized that it could run into a good deal of money, flying people around the country to attend the services of candidates. Delegates might have come all the way by car to New Sharon in a day, but as Hilda explained when he met her, long auto trips gave her severe back pain. If Epiphany was looking into finalists farther afield, and Andrews allowed that possibility, committee expenses would be zooming. This kind of congregation would search coast to coast for a suitable minister. The committee had sent a copy of the current church budget. It was large. But the five thousand allocated to "pastoral search" would not allow for many junkets by air. Andrews hoped that figure was not meant to include the new pastor's moving expenses.

After receiving Jim's letter, Andrews had tried in vain to visualize Hilda Cox and Harry Bauman. He suspected they might vary in age and interest. One of them might even be a teenager. It was common for a representative of the youth fellowship to serve on such a committee. And it might be a shrewd move to have a youth member check out a doddering candidate. But he was only speculating. The committee would send whoever was available on a particular date. There was no way of knowing.

Unfortunately September 15 was the day Sunday school opened after summer recess. The superintendent and one of the teachers would be making announcements, and Andrews had very little control over how long they might take or how tedious their remarks might be. He always found that particular Sunday of the year pretty much a bore himself. The second graders would be presented with Bibles, and the names on the cradle roll would be read aloud. He hoped the Epiphany visitors would not find all of it too hokey.

Andrews had also been concerned about the choir. They had only practiced once since May. Andrews took pride in his choir. He believed them to be above average for a church of that size and setting. But they were likely to be short-handed and rusty. Fortunately the choir director had decided to have them sing something they had done many times before. It was a simple arrangement of the hymn "All Creatures of Our God and King." A good tune, and they ought to be able to handle it.

And what about his sermon? Usually on this particular Sunday of the year, he would speak rather briefly about Sunday school. But that wouldn't give the visitors much insight into his preaching. As outsiders they were likely to find the whole service tiresome. On the other hand, wasn't the delegation coming to get a feel for what his ministry was like on the inside? They ought to be. And Christian education was something their own church profile stressed.

It was hard to know, but he decided to preach a sermon that avoided local shop talk and was inspirational in theme. He would take as his text Peter 2:9: "For you are a royal priesthood . . ." He thought he could cover the right bases with that, including Christian education. It was a passage he had preached before, but he would try to bring a fresh approach. Let the Spirit lead.

There was one good thing about the delegation coming on that particular day. Because of the opening of Sunday school, there would be a good attendance. Weather cooperating.

The evening before the service, Andrews had done

something he hadn't tried for many years, though in the beginning it was part of his regular routine. He went into the chancel and practiced his sermon. The church was dark except for the light on the pulpit, though ever so often the headlights of passing cars would illumine the stained glass windows. In the old days, in his first little parish in Iowa, he would imagine certain members of his congregation sitting there in the darkness, and he would direct his thoughts to them individually. That seemed to make his sermon come more to life. He often revised his manuscript afterwards as a result. But that night in September, he could not visualize Hilda Cox or Harry Bauman. And the whole time he stood there, he was afraid someone would come into the church and catch him in the act.

The following morning he walked into the chancel during the organ prelude, trying to look as if he were not looking for the visitor's faces. Over the years he had developed the art of reading aloud and even of speaking extemporaneously while thinking of something else. It was an art he called upon as he began leading the responsive psalm. Every time his eyes looked up from the page, he searched the faces of the congregation. He read aloud and searched and, as he did these two things, he was conscious of doing both, which meant, he told himself, that his mind was engaged in three activities. Four, really, because his telling himself that it was so was still another activity. And of that, too, he was aware. He was aware of himself reading aloud while looking for the Epiphany visitors, aware of that awareness, and so on ad infinitum. His mind was infinite, another observation transcending all previous ones. His mind was perpetually self-transcending, and in that realization as much as anything, he supposed, lay the divine image. All those high and expansive thoughts came to him as he read his lines in a clear, bright, uplifting tone, while searching for those two strange faces.

"What is man that thou art mindful of him, and the son of man that thou dost care for him?"

Andrews answered: "Yet thou has made him little less than sheep and oxen, and also the beasts of the field."

But he had skipped something. Did anyone notice? How could they help but notice? Yet they were regulars, most of them, journeymen responders, and had skipped ahead with a smoothness that was remarkable. Andrews' mind was infinite then, but not infallible. What saved him from getting lost entirely was something fixed in him, yet so high that it transcended everything else, even his pretensions to infinity. It was that high eye of laughter looking back at himself. That laughter, he knew, was where his soul touched God. The laughter was not showing, though. It rarely did. He concluded the psalm with such sober poise that no one but himself remembered that anything had gone wrong.

As he turned the page and gazed out over the congregation, he finally spotted two strangers.

After the service, he found Hilda Cox and Harry Bauman waiting in a corner. They were oddly matched. Hilda Cox appeared to be in her late sixties. A tall, serene widow, she told Andrews she had been a member of

Epiphany Church since she came to the area as a bride. Her husband, Neil, had taught in the engineering school at the university. For the last twenty years of his life, he had chaired the building and grounds committee at the church. He had lived just long enough, Hilda told Andrews, her eyes filling, to supervise the installation of an automated heating system.

Harry Bauman was a very tall man in his early thirties, so fair that even his eyebrows were platinum blond. A frown excavated his forehead whenever he was called upon to think, so Andrews hesitated to say anything serious in his presence for fear of subjecting him to too much strain. Harry had grown up in Epiphany Church, but he confessed to Andrews that he had not been at all active until asked to join the search committee. It was a responsibility he assumed earnestly.

"Harry started on the 1976 basketball team," Hilda told Andrews right after he encountered them hovering by the literature rack. "That was the one that made the NCAA quarterfinals."

Given his complexion, Harry's blush was dramatic.

"What do you do now?" Andrews asked.

"I'm a sales representative," he answered. Whom he represented, he did not say.

Andrews was disappointed. He had geared himself for a more academic pair. But it was easy to relax with them. He and Kate had debated whether they should ask the delegation for dinner at the parsonage. Would that be expected, or would it be presumptuous under the circumstances? They decided in the end that they would play it by ear. Kate would join her husband in greeting the Epiphany people after the service. If it developed that they just wanted to talk with the candidate for a few minutes in a businesslike way, Kate would go home, and Andrews would take Hilda and Harry to his study at the church. If they suggested going out for lunch, Andrews would either accept the invitation or invite them to the parsonage depending on how he felt they would react. Meanwhile, Kate would have a lunch in readiness.

As it turned out, it seemed the most natural thing in the world for Kate to invite Hilda and Harry to the parsonage.

"It will just be a simple lunch," she told them. "But I'm sure you'll find it more comfortable and easier to talk there. The choice of restaurants in New Sharon is limited, and after church on Sunday they are overflowing."

Andrews thought the gathering at the parsonage went rather well. Kate had prepared a chicken salad that earned the praise of heavy consumption. But Hilda and Harry did not stay long; they were anxious about making their return flight in Madison. Both told Andrews that they liked his sermon and were impressed by the spirit of enthusiasm shown by his church school. They wished they could say the same for their own. The minister of Christian education resigned when Dr. Goodens retired. The seminary student they brought in as a temporary replacement was not very effective. On the whole, Andrews reflected afterwards, the meeting was, in diplomatic jargon, cordial but not substantive. There was only one question that continued to haunt him:

"What led to your decision to go into the ministry?" Hilda had asked.

Andrews had not anticipated that question. After all, he had been a minister for more than thirty years, and though sometimes he wondered whether he ought to get out of it, he rarely asked himself how he got into it. He heard himself responding vaguely, "There came a moment when I was still in college when everything seemed to point me that way."

The answer was true enough as far as it went. It seemed to satisfy Hilda. Afterwards he chided himself. He had given an answer that went nowhere at all.

For the next several nights the question kept him awake. Why did he become a minister? It certainly was not a fashionable calling among the crowd he grew up with. No one among his early friends went on to don the cloth. Most, in fact, had declared themselves agnostic by the eighth grade, although, he noted, later on, when married and with a child or two, they usually drifted into some sort of church. The early 1950s was a great era of church building among people of his generation, especially in the newer suburbs. Although many urban and rural churches were dying, religious leaders shrugged off these losses as due to changing population patterns. In the suburbs, where it counted, especially the vast new residential tracts that blossomed after World War II, new church buildings were going up everywhere, dominated by elaborate Christian education plants. It was just at this time that he entered theological school. His classmates and professors ceaselessly excoriated the shallowness of the religious boom. But they were happy enough, Andrews observed, to ride its crest.

"You people will have it easy," one of his homiletics professors declared, a man who had spent thirty years in a historic pulpit on Fifth Avenue. "For my generation, it was an uphill struggle all the way. War, disillusionment, skepticism, and then the Depression. Don't let anyone tell you the Great Depression was good for the soul. But for you fellows the road leads to better things."

Not for long, Andrews reflected. Not for his kind of church. He had lost touch with most of his early friends, but he suspected that, by the time their children left high school, most had fallen into the inactive church rolls. And he doubted that their children went back to church after they were grown. Those big educational plants were now rented out as daycare centers or as meeting halls for Weight Watchers.

Reflecting on his early days, he could not think of any influence that might have prodded him toward the ministry. In later years, he constantly ran into people who asked him if his grandfather was a minister. There seemed to be a commonly held belief that the ministry ran in families. Perhaps people found it hard to believe that anyone would become a minister unless the calling was an inherited characteristic, the result of some gene.

In any case, his own father was far from being a clergyman. His father's family had belonged to a church, but their participation was minimal, and Andrews had never heard his grandparents express any religious views. Nor his father, either, so far as he could recall. His father did join a neighborhood church in the older Eastern suburb where Andrews was raised, the kind with sidewalks and a main street that developed when railroads came out from the city just after the Civil War. He even served as an usher. When Andrews was very young, the ushers still wore morning coats and striped trousers, and his father looked very distinguished leading the ladies with their feathered hats down the center aisle, a fresh white carnation pinned to his lapel. Even though he performed that service cheerfully, his father never showed much interest in the church itself. When Andrews told him of his decision to go to seminary, his father reacted with puzzlement and a quiet disappointment. Though his native courtesy kept him from saying so directly, it was clear that he had hoped for something better from his only son.

Andrews' mother had been mildly pleased. It was she who saw to it that he began attending Sunday school at an early age. In a real sense, he had grown up in that suburban church, a large institution with a heritage going back to colonial times. In Andrew's childhood, the church had boasted a large congregation, a massive building of blue stone, three clergy, and a full-time minister of music. The senior pastor, Dr. Longworth, was a workmanlike and scholarly preacher, amazingly well read, considering all his activities, and always attuned to contemporary events. Of course, Dr. Longworth spent ten weeks every summer in Maine where he could do the kind of sustained reading and sermon preparation that Andrews never found time to do. Despite his church's Puritan heritage, Dr. Longworth inclined to liturgical worship. Andrews still looked back with admiration to the grandeur of those Advent and Easter services.

But he could not say that Dr. Longworth had had much to do with his decision to go into the ministry. Somewhere in his files there was a letter from his old pastor congratulating him on his ordination: "How thrilling, Jack, to hear from your mother of this great event!" The hearty exclamation point forested the letters of clergymen of that era.

Andrews could not recall ever discussing the ministry with Dr. Longworth. He could not recall having discussed anything important with Dr. Longworth at all. It was hard to say what in his background nudged him toward the ministry. As he thought about it, he realized that the decision came toward the end of what he had come to describe as the "hard years," beginning with his father's business failure. His father had headed a small but highly respected import firm established by Andrews' grandfather at the turn of the century. The Depression and the war must have had something to do with the loss of business. But his father took the collapse of the firm as a personal failure, compounded by the feeling that he had let his own father down. The old man was dead by then, but that didn't seem to matter. Andrews' father had dropped the baton, and though he later became an officer in another company, he never recovered. Defeat clung to him for the rest of his life like the scent of spent cigars that pervaded his den at home.

One result of the reversal in the family finances was that Andrews had been forced to come home from boarding school halfway through his sophomore year and begin attending the local high school. On the whole, he found that a welcome change. And after so many years at boy's schools, he was glad to meet a few girls. He never felt quite at ease with them, but they were there on a daily basis for him to look at and talk about, and that was a big advantage.

But something in him began to unravel. The atmosphere at home was depressing. His father grew increasingly melancholy and remote. His mother took refuge in a group that held meetings in a local hotel. Its members were devoted to "imagineering" and positive thinking. Andrews' sister, who was two years younger than he, became so erratic in her behavior that the school counselor recommended she sit out a semester while receiving psychiatric help. Instead, his parents sent her to a special school for disturbed children. The decision placed a new strain on the family's resources.

Another result of his family's worsened financial position was that Andrews could not attend what his parents considered to be a "good college"—an Ivy League school or one of the more prestigious small liberal arts institutions. His grades had begun to decline while he was still at boarding school. He did moderately well at the public high school, but he was unable to win a scholarship. His father talked of selling the house to make it possible for Andrews to attend one of the colleges whose catalogs he had collected. His SAT scores were probably high enough for him to get in, if he were able to pay his way. But for the first time, Andrews asserted himself with his parents. Without their knowing, he took a bus to Bradford State College and enrolled.

Andrews had no definite vocational plans when he started college. He decided to major in American history for no other reason than that he found the subject interesting. He thought about going to law school when he graduated. His parents would have liked that. But he could not say he felt any enthusiasm for the law or any other profession. He was stirred by vague longings, but he cherished no particular goals. His mother told him to be patient and he would find himself. But as he moved into his junior year, he feared that time was running out, that his "self" had permanently slipped away. Like two or three of his friends who were equally at a loss, he considered military service. But Andrews had already failed his draft physical because of a punctured eardrum. It was the only thing, he used to say, that he had in common with Frank Sinatra.

He could not say that he showed much interest in religion in those days. There was no religious studies program at Bradford. As a state school, the college steered clear of anything sectarian, though that policy posed no barrier to the professor in Philosophy 101 who attacked Christianity at every turn. A counter-attack emerged through a campus minister representing several denominations that held meetings in an old house at the edge of the campus. He was a tweedy, pipe-smoking man in his late thirties, who called all the students "gal" and "fella." He seemed to enjoy hanging out in a local beer hall, drinking Schlitz, and discussing Kierkegaard. Andrews didn't care much for the minister or his ideas. But he did begin reading Kierkegaard.

About halfway through his junior year, Andrews began

visiting various churches in the area. The previous year he had lived at home to save money, but with his parents' encouragement he'd moved into a dormitory so that he could spend less time commuting and more time participating in campus life. He started going to church on Sunday mornings because nothing else was going on and he felt lonely.

Most of the services bored him, but one Sunday in April he dropped in on a small church on the edge of town. Twice a month, after the service, the church served a soup luncheon. The church was a denomination other than his own, but as soon as he walked through the door he felt at home. He enjoyed the soup luncheons, even though sometimes he was the only one (except for Pastor Pringle and his wife) under the age of seventy. Everyone seemed so pleased to have him there. The pastor was a man of about forty who had a knack for preaching sermons with themes seemingly simple enough for the opening exercises of the Sunday school. And yet despite their apparent simplicity, those sermons always set Andrews thinking. He was reminded of the little tunes in a Beethoven symphony that grew enwebbed in patterns of massive profundity—or in another way, of a Robert Frost poem that he had been tempted to dismiss as a bit of folksy doggerel until he realized it opened up to meanings on many subtle levels. Pastor Pringle was not intellectual in the manner of Dr. Longworth. He never quoted St. Augustine or Reinhold Niebuhr, or for that matter, Hemingway or J.P. Marquand. He rarely quoted anybody outside the Bible. But he had an original cast of mind that could bring astonishing trains of thought out of the dullest biblical text. The year that Andrews graduated from Bradford, Pastor Pringle moved to Ohio. Andrews never heard anything about him after that. Yet for the rest of his life, he would tell his colleagues that Herman Pringle was one of the greatest preachers of his generation.

During the summer between his junior and senior years, Andrews had a job working at a resort hotel in northern New Hampshire, an enormous relic of the last century with multiple turrets and a long veranda that overhung a lake lined with boulders. Rusticity and elegance, tradition and youth, romance and domesticity combined in a special blend that Andrews found satisfying at the time, and to which, in reminiscence, he had applied a rich varnish on all the summers since. While a large share of the clientele was elderly couples and forlorn widows who had been coming every summer for decades, the resort was still popular with younger families who could afford the high rates. A steady schedule of organized children's activities left parents free to enjoy themselves.

That was how Kate came to be there. She was one of the several girls from Vassar assigned to guide the children's program. Andrews was in charge of canoe rentals, doubled as a bell hop, and sometimes led groups on hikes. In the evenings, after the children were in bed, the college kids danced to a jukebox in a recreation hall located in a building behind the hotel. The first time Andrews danced with Kate, he cut in on a friend from Bradford. Though cutting in was common enough, Kate had never met him before, and she seemed startled.

"Well now," she exclaimed, "and who might you be?"

"John Mason Andrews," he said, "at your service."

For the next three minutes he could not think of anything else to say. As the song came to an end, and a new record slid into place in the jukebox, Kate told him, "I take it John Mason Andrews is the strong silent type."

"Only silent. My knees are like mush."

"Are you always that way, or is it only when you're dancing?"

"Oh, I can be quite talkative. It's just that I'm struck dumb by your beauty."

Kate leaned away from him as if in alarm. Before he could speak again, someone else cut in. It was just as well, he thought afterwards. He could not imagine what to say next. But he had established a connection.

The next morning Andrews made a point of finding Kate again, this time in the staff dining room. He picked up his tray at the end of the cafeteria line and walked right over to where she was having breakfast. In retrospect his boldness surprised him, but there was something about Kate that dispelled his diffidence. From the very beginning he was at ease with Kate. He was telling the truth when he told her she was beautiful. Kate was tall with dark hair down to her shoulders and eyes so deeply blue that he thought they were brown until he saw them up close. Her wide brow might have disqualified her as a fashion model. But in its breadth Andrews found something wise and welcoming.

Andrews was glad that he and Kate were companions

long before they were lovers. From the very beginning they were friends, and though their relationship grew more intense over time, it never outgrew the lighthearted spirit with which it began. The love that emerged rose out of their mutual laughter. Kate often mocked him, especially when he was overly self-conscious and tried desperately to say something clever. But she never humiliated him. Even her mockery was affirming. There was understanding in her laughter. There was respect. When Andrews was with Kate, he was not only at ease with her. He was at ease with himself.

More than once through the years, Andrews pondered the connection between his meeting Kate and the other great event that took place in his life that summer. He had come to learn that sex and religion intermingled in myriad ways. Early in his ministry, he witnessed the closing ceremonies of church youth camps in which boys and girls marched into the night singing, "Follow the Gleam." Along with the other counselors, he had to spend the rest of the night patrolling the grounds. He had fielded from the pulpit the adoring glances of old ladies and of some not so old. He knew that the steady glow that enveloped him that summer in New Hampshire was tinted with many lights, not all of which shone directly from the heavens. But he refused to believe that the call that came to him one day was any less genuine because he heard it while falling in love with Kate. On the contrary, he considered his falling in love a means of grace. The Spirit of God did not work in a vacuum. The Spirit reached out through all the experiences of a person's life. As he began to envision a future with Kate in it, he started to face up to his need to formulate some definite vocational goals. More important, in Kate he found someone who accepted him despite his imperfections. The acceptance was liberating. He began to believe that his life held important possibilities. Without Kate's acceptance, he doubted that he could have believed in God's acceptance, or that God might have some task for him to try.

Near the end of his time at the summer hotel, Andrews was asked to lead some of the older children on a hike to a small lake about a mile away. He decided to walk the trail in advance so that he would know what to expect. The trail led him through a thick stand of dark spruce and pine. Though he walked at a brisk place, his feet fell silently on the matted needles. He kept feeling that he was approaching a dark precipice that any moment would cast him headlong into the future in an irreversible fall.

Earlier that summer his father had tried to engage Andrews in a serious talk about his future. He would graduate from Bradford the next year. His father perceived that his son was not committed to the idea of going to law school and suggested that Andrews apply to Harvard Business School.

"I think you can get in," his father had told him. "I have a friend on the faculty—you remember Dr. Keane—and we had lunch together the other day. I told him that your grades at the state college are quite good, and Dr. Keane suggested that you make an appointment to see him sometime early in the fall."

Andrews did not want to disappoint his father or to appear ungrateful. He agreed to phone Dr. Keane for an appointment early in the fall. But he dreaded going to see the man. Andrews was not in the least attracted to business school.

During his summer in New Hampshire, the thought came to him of becoming a forest ranger. He loved the wilderness and he had done well in the few biology courses that he had taken. He mentioned the idea to Kate, and though she shared his interest in the outdoors, she was dubious. She told him that no matter how much he liked trees, he was somebody who needed to work with ideas and with people. She was like that herself, she said. She could not imagine herself spending her life atop a fire tower. As Andrews drew near the end of the trail, he admitted to himself that Kate was probably right.

Suddenly he was out of the wood and facing the lake. The sugar maples on the opposite shore were beginning to turn. He was surprised at how isolated the place was. There was not a single cabin in sight. He stepped out onto a rocky ledge. A great blue heron rose up below him, flew to the other side, and landed in a patch of reeds. The heron squeezed itself into a motionless eye. As Andrews looked out over the water, it seemed as though all his senses were heightened. He could see a nuthatch creeping upside down on a distant tree trunk; he could hear the threshing wings of a pair of mating dragon flies; he could smell the ripening cattails on the far shore. He was alone here. This was his place. He shuddered at the thought of sharing it with a crowd of noisy seventh graders. He wanted no one here with him, except possibly Kate. And then, for reasons he could not explain, he began thinking about Pastor Pringle and the soup luncheons. And then of Christ. And of Simon and Andrew by another lake. And he knew he was called.

Afterwards, it would make Andrews angry when a speaker at a clergy meeting would suggest that one's call to the ministry may only have been the mince pie one had for dinner. Even at the time when he had come to doubt everything else, Andrews never doubted that something decisive and transcendent had happened to him on the shore of the little lake with the turning maples.

But how could he speak of his experience to someone like Hilda Cox or Harry Bauman? How could he explain the experience to anyone?

# CHAPTER SIX

Sue Grant stood just beyond the security checkpoint a Gate 3, waiting for Flight 301 to empty its passengers into the far shadows of the long corridor. The screen above her displayed the news that the plane was on the ground, but it always seemed an eternity from when a plane pulled up to the gate and when the flight attendants opened the door. She wished Hilda Cox hadn't run off at the last minute and left her with this assignment. Fortunately, she had no afternoon classes, but she did have other things planned. She had reconciled herself to the fact that Friday evening, as well as most of Saturday and Sunday, would be taken up by another candidate visit. But she had counted on having Friday afternoon to herself, and now that was shot. If she had known how much time this pastoral search business was going to take, she would never have consented to serve on the committee. She still could not believe that she had agreed to be secretary. As a matter of principle, she had long ago decided never to be secretary of anything. And yet here she was. Why didn't they make Curtiss Myrick secretary? It was just the job for an old boy like him.

She supposed the fact that she was secretary had something to do with Kelly coming into her office last week. She still didn't know what to make of that; it was outrageous. She was so mad she made a phone call, marched right out of her office and down to the coffee shop to meet Patti Leone. Sue expected Patti to go off like a bomb. And Patti had been angry, though not entirely surprised. Patti was in administration for the university and had experienced almost everything.

"Now what's this all about?" Patti had asked. "You look like you've just been bitten by a snake."

"You hit the nail on the head," Sue had replied. "The snake is Kelly, my division head."

"You mean Cyrus Kelly?"

"That's right, 'Cyrus the Mede' Kelly. He came into that little cubby hole they call my office, sat down on one corner of my desk, and said he'd heard I was one of the 'powers' on the search committee at Epiphany Church. I told him I was on the committee, but hardly a power."

"Oh, but you are, Sue, you're the secretary," Patti said.

They both laughed. Patti had been absent the day the committee made Sue the secretary, or it never would have happened. Patti was Epiphany's resident feminist.

"Sure, I'm a power. I'm also a lowly assistant professor of art, which makes me easier to influence than somebody like you or Paul. Kelly hasn't approached you, has he?"

"No. What about?"

"About the Reverend Maria Shilling of New York, who Kelly understood to be one of our final candidates. I thought we'd done a pretty good job of keeping the names confidential. But here's Kelly, who's not even a member of our church, bringing up Maria's name."

Patti shook her head. "Things get around," she said. "Could be that Kelly heard about it from somebody who knows Shilling."

"Probably," Sue agreed. "But Kelly seems to know a lot about what we've been doing. He said he'd heard I was one of those sponsoring Maria." She had to pause a moment. She tried to mask her emotion by taking a bite of her Danish roll. "I told Kelly," she said carefully, "that I wasn't sponsoring anybody. I said that we were checking out a number of candidates and that I'd been assigned, along with someone else—I didn't say who—to meet with Maria in New York. But that didn't mean I was promoting her. I said we were still looking at candidates."

Patti looked amused. "And what did Cyrus say?"

"He said he wanted me to know there was someone high up in the administration who thought very highly of Maria Shilling and that he hoped I would use my influence to see that she was given every consideration."

Patti's eyebrows ventured toward the edge of her hairline. "And who might this person be?"

"I don't know. I got the impression it might have been President McGrath himself. But how would he know Maria, I wonder?"

Patti took a sip from her coffee. "May not know her at all, but he may know somebody important who does. And that character, whoever it is, has been in touch with McGrath. If it is McGrath. Or one of the vice presidents. Who knows? They call it networking. I've got other names for it."

"But why doesn't this high-up person speak for himself?" Sue asked.

"Doesn't want to get involved directly," Patti said. "After all, this is a state school. It wouldn't look right."

"But he sent Kelly to talk to me."

Patti grunted. "Yeah. Right. So what did you tell him?"

"Well, I was getting a little annoyed. I told Kelly that I felt whoever this high-up administrator was should speak for himself, write a letter to the committee, or call Jim Purdy. I didn't like this round-about, cloak-and-dagger way doing things."

"Good for you!" Patti put down her cup with a bang.

"Maybe not so good. Kelly started getting paternal then, and saying that I needed to understand how the world worked. Along the way he let something drop about my coming up for tenure next year."

Then Patti got mad. She even suggested calling in the ACLU until Sue quieted her down. Before they went back to work, the women agreed not to say anything to the rest of the committee. It might hurt Maria's chances. As Patti said,

Maria probably didn't know anything about Cyrus Kelly. She just had a friend who thought he'd put in a good word for her. But the whole intrigue put a bad taste in Sue's mouth. She had actually been a supporter of Maria Shilling before. She wasn't sure anymore.

Sue looked at her watch. She had been standing by Gate 3 for half an hour. How was she to know the man she waited for?

Hilda said Reverend Andrews looked a little younger than he really was, that he was tall, had a rather long face, and wore glasses. A dolichocephalic, northern European, far-sighted male in his fifties. Not exactly a rare commodity in the upper Midwest. The description fit Cyrus Kelly, in fact.

Of course, Sue did have a sign with "Epiphany" in large letters. The lettering had been done by one of her students in the sort of luminous reddish-orange worn by highway survey crews. From a distance, the Gothic script offered more in flamboyance than in clarity. She would hold up the sign only as a last resort.

The advance contingent of passengers exiting the plane appeared in the distance: a uniformed airport employee pushing a woman in a wheelchair, followed by a man with two small girls. In a moment, others emerged. Forging past the wheelchair were business-types with assorted brief cases and carry-on luggage. Next came a swarm of young males, students probably, uniformed in blue jeans, sweatshirts, and baseball caps stuck on backwards. There was a gap—no one in sight. For an instant it seemed that the Reverend John Mason Andrews had missed the plane. Might he have changed his mind? She felt deserted. Something sharp turned inside her, something akin to grief.

But then another knot of passengers appeared, including a tall, fiftyish man in a light gray business suit, a man with a look of such command that he need not shore up his authority with darkness. He was nice-looking, distinguished, attractive despite his age. As he came near, Sue smiled. "Mr. Andrews?"

The man walked by, extending his hand to a professional looking woman in a suit of navy blue. And then, pressing by, charged a surge of men, similarly dressed. They were legion, especially on airplanes; they were the world conspiracy, the powers and principalities. Why had Hilda Cox gone off and left her at their mercy?

She clamped her teeth and held up the sign. Immediately a man who had been standing to one side, smiled shyly and came toward her. Surprised, she froze for an instant, her mouth open. No wonder she had missed him. He wasn't wearing glasses.

As Andrews exited the jetway and stepped into the terminal, he had ignored the rather small young woman with dark hair pulled into a sort of bun. He had expected that one of the people who came to New Sharon would meet him, probably Mrs. Cox, the widowed lady, the one who wanted to know why he had decided to become a minister. When he started to look around for a familiar face, he began to regret that he had taken off his glasses. It was just that he felt surer of his footing without them, especially if called upon to use an escalator. And if any of the committee whom he had not met were here to greet him, he would just as soon not make a trifocular first impression. As a result he was lost. Then he saw the Epiphany sign. He was saved.

But why did the young woman look so startled? Was his fly open? He shifted his garment bag to his other shoulder so he could check.

"Mr. Andrews?" the woman said.

Shifting the garment bag again, he took her hand, small and firm, within his own.

"I'm Sue Grant," she told him. "Hilda was going to meet you, but she was called away on some emergency. So I'm doing the honors." Coming from that diminutive, rather tense figure, the voice was unexpected. The tone was high, clear, round, the voice from an Edith Wharton novel.

"Well, I'm very grateful that you came." He looked down at her benignly. A thin, sensitive face, he thought, intellectual, but at the same time, sensual. He had read somewhere in college that, contrary to expectations, ectomorphs were often the most erotic. Which was no doubt an outdated concept. Certainly at this moment an inappropriate recollection.

"May I take your bags?"

In addition to the garment bag, he carried an oversized attaché case, containing not only his sermon and various other papers, but his fresh socks and underwear. In the garment bag were his pulpit robe, his best suit, two neckties, several shirts, a raincoat, and an extra pair of pants. He would have liked to have been relieved of the attaché case, to have more freedom for handling the unwieldy garment bag. But no one-hundred-six-pound woman was going to carry something of his, even if she were his junior by twenty years. Then that high eye in himself laughed and asked whether he did not have that the wrong way around. Perhaps if the woman were twenty years older, he would have let her carry all his baggage. He smiled.

She was staring at him. "Did I say something funny?"

"No. Not at all." He smiled again. "Thanks for the offer, but I'll carry both items. Having one on either side helps me keep in balance."

Sue Grant drove Andrews to a motel near the university, pointing out along the way a high school, a hospital, and a low-income housing complex that Epiphany Church had helped to sponsor. It was not a large city, yet he was struck, almost cowed, by the contrast to New Sharon. The speed of the traffic, the wideness of the streets, the size and modernity of the buildings intimidated him. He was in the habit of traveling to Madison and Milwaukee. Occasionally he drove to Chicago. He moved within those urban settings as a mere visitor. The cities demanded nothing of him. He always went home again to his familiar little place. But he would be expected to measure up to this city, and if he came here to live, he could not escape.

As the car turned onto a broad avenue paralleling the university, Andrews felt as if he were about to succumb to an anxiety attack. The wild auto traffic was alarming enough, but he could not recall when he had seen such mobs afoot. The walkers were not forging ahead as in most places, eyes locked on their destinations. They were constantly shouting to one another and forming moving clusters that changed continually in size and shape. There was a festive air about the street with its cappucino bars, bookstores, and outdoor displays of decorated T-shirts.

*Look carefully how you walk . . . for the days are evil.* Words in a letter.

"Here we are," Sue announced.

Andrews looked out to see a pair of golden doors. He must be in Oz. The lobby, though, looked and smelled much like any other motel. Sue checked at the desk to make sure the reservation was in order.

"I'll be going now," she told him. "Someone is scheduled to pick you up at six—it might be Jim Purdy—and take you to dinner." She looked at her watch, smiled quickly, and went outside through the golden doors.

Andrews looked down at his own watch. Four-fifteen. Time for a shower and a change of clothes and a moment of quiet to put his head in order. Suddenly he felt very tired. He was glad the committee had taken it for granted he would come by air. He picked up his key and his luggage and went in search of his room.

As soon as he threw down his bags, he went to the window and pulled back the drapes. Though he wanted this trip to remain secret, Kate had slipped and told her mother about it on the phone. Half an hour later, Kate's mother had called back to say that her friend Eloise had reported that Andrews would be traveling to a lovely little city, noted for its brick and ivy campus and its wide avenues flanked by horse chestnut trees. No sign of a horse chestnut out there. No trees at all. Only the back side of a supermarket.

He stood in the dressing area outside the bathroom and looked at his face in the mirror. So far it seemed to be in reasonably good order. But it looked out of place. It was a face respected in New Sharon, a transient face in the eyes of the natives, a "passing guest," to use an expression from the RSV, but the face of a person of some importance. People would be sorry to see it go. He would be sorry. And the sorrow would show in his eyes, giving him away to any new faces that might look into his.

He stepped back and began to remove his necktie. Why was he putting himself through his ordeal? There was no necessity for him to go through the indignity of offering himself for sale to strangers. And what if the sale were completed? He could see no further than the soiled loading dock of a supermarket.

The Bend in the River restaurant may not have served the best food in town, but it was the most popular, a highly successful establishment founded and operated by two former students who had dropped out of the university MBA program after failing a course in management. In design and decor, The Bend was original. The tables were replicas of ancient lecture hall desks with attached chairs. Sugar sat in inkwells. Along the walls, between the leather-bound volumes, were photographs of campus luminaries. Not athletic heroes, as might be expected, but faculty. Each photograph had a brass label underneath, bearing the professor's name, campus sobriquet, subject taught, and years with the university. The Bend was not a student hangout, but it was the place where students brought their parents when their parents were paying. University faculty favored the restaurant for entertaining accreditation teams. And the Epiphany Church search committee had chosen it for their Friday evening dinners with each of the final four candidates.

Until the main course was served, Andrews found the atmosphere relaxed, even jovial. Hilda Cox and Harry Bauman greeted him like an old friend. They gave him the feeling that he was their man. Whether he was or not, he must have passed muster with them or he would not be dining at The Bend. Those whom he had not met before welcomed him cordially and went out of their way to avoid giving the impression that they were looking him over. They talked pleasantly with him about his trip. No one tried to talk with him exclusively. In fact, at one point three or four separate conversations broke out simultaneously, none of which had anything to do with the Reverend John Mason Andrews or Epiphany Church. Andrews felt himself escaping into anonymity. He was beginning to think that he might get through this dinner without having to pass any test at all. So long as his table manners were satisfactory, he had it made.

Then, just as he began to cut into his roast beef, a silence fell. It was one of those silences that radiated conspiracy. He sensed that in the silence all the diners had come together, all but himself. He looked up from his plate rather regretfully. Was someone asking him a question?

Yes, Jim Purdy.

"We were saying, Jack, that our last pastor always avoided preaching about stewardship. How do you feel about that?"

Andrews put his knife down slowly. He would be careful. It was best not to cut down former pastors. "If you mean by stewardship, asking for money, that's a sensitive matter. Our pastors don't want to appear like some of those TV evangelists calling for contributions in every other breath."

"Send in your request today for your free Bible verse key-chain," Harry Bauman said, "and by the way, you might enclose a check."

Andrews looked at Harry and smiled. "Yes. That kind of thing gives all churches a bad image. But if we mean by stewardship . . ."

"Isn't that a euphemism, really?" It was the intense professor-type with the beard. They had been introduced, but Andrews could not recall the man's name.

"I admit the word does become a euphemism much of the time. But I believe it has a genuine meaning. There's a biblical base to it, after all. Stewardship means caring for God's world and employing our talents and resources effectively in God's service. That is something I think we should preach about. And the church figures into that. People do need to be reminded of their commitment to the church, a commitment that includes financial support. Although some people don't like it, I do make it a practice to talk about stewardship in that sense. I don't do it all the time, but at least once a year I try to challenge people to take financial responsibility for the work of the church, both locally and world-wide."

Jim Purdy leaned back with a look of satisfaction. He said quietly, "I think that's part of a pastor's job."

People began eating again. But there was very little conversation, and Jack sensed that heavier questions might be on their way.

After a time, Hilda cleared her throat. As if on cue, knives and forks were set down. "One of the issues . . ." Hilda started to say more, but there was a frog in her throat and she reached for her water glass. "One of the issues before the church today," she continued, "has to do with the rights of homosexuals. I wonder how you feel, Reverend Andrews, about the church where you might be . . ." She cleared her throat again. "A church where you were pastor, adopting an open . . ." Hilda seemed to lose her composure. A look of panic came into her normally comfortable eyes.

"An open and affirming policy toward gays and lesbians," the woman wearing a black dress spoke the words loudly enough for the whole restaurant to hear.

Patti Leone. Andrews remembered her name. Brash, direct, confrontational. She frightened him.

"If you have in mind my present situation," he said quietly, "I must say that it would not happen. There is no way my church would adopt such a policy officially. My people aren't ready for that." He knew what he said was true, though he knew as well that people in New Sharon were protective of their own. No gay or lesbian already in the church would be challenged.

"But suppose you went to another church where the issue was raised," Patti said, "and some individual or group of members brought forward an open and affirming resolution. How would you feel?"

With hardly a thought, he answered, "I'd be scared as hell."

To his relief, everyone laughed. Patti laughed louder than any of the others. Still, she pressed him.

"But what's your opinion on the subject?"

He should have expected something like this. In a place like this. But like his people back home, Andrews was not ready. He asked, "Have you adopted such a resolution here?"

"No," Hilda said quickly.

"Not yet," Patti corrected her. "But it could happen soon."

Andrews met the large woman's gaze. "You have to realize," he said slowly, "that I was brought up in a world where this matter was never mentioned." He looked toward Hilda for confirmation, but her eyes were turned away. "Or rarely mentioned. Once or twice at college, the subject came up. There were certain people that we suspected . . . There were jokes . . ." How could he get his mind back on track? "What I mean to say is that when I went into the ministry, and until quite recently, the thought of the church going out of its way to welcome gays and lesbians was about as acceptable as the church sending out an invitation to pimps and child molesters." He paused at the sound of his own words. "I'm being frank . . . I'm . . ."

Maybe he had gone too far. No heads nodded in affirmation. Their faces were stones.

Paul Knudson—Andrews had the name—regarded the candidate sternly. "Times change," he said.

"I know that, Dr. Knudson. I'm only saying how sudden this about-face in cultural attitudes strikes people like me." He was sinking deeper. Why did he keep reminding the committee how long he had been around?

He tried again. "I only want to say that for someone with my background, it is hard to be entirely comfortable with this subject. And I may add that such discomfort exists for most of our ministers, regardless of age, though some may not be honest enough to admit it. There's a lot of deception, a lot of self-deception, on this issue and other questions in the church these days."

Andrews would be forthright now. But he must try not to grow defensive, combative. "One part of me, and I sincerely hope it is the better part, says that homo . . . gays and lesbians have the same right to share in the life of the church as anyone else. And not to hide who they are either. But there is also that other part of me, a part formed by a spiritual heritage going back many centuries, that feels, well, ill at ease."

"A fifties upbringing," Sue Grant said.

She had struck one of his points of irritation: the attribution of every cramped standard to that single decade.

"You flatter me," he told her. "I was pretty well formed before the fifties came along. The truth is that these old attitudes were there in the forties, the thirties, and right back through all the centuries of our Judeo-Christian tradition."

The committee member named Mark, the one who Andrews recalled saying something earlier about studying for the ministry, leaned forward. "You think there are biblical grounds then for opposing homosexuality?"

"I didn't say that." Andrews knew that people were writing books arguing to the contrary. He wished that he had read one. "I'm only saying," he spoke deliberately, "that there are some long-standing feelings on the subject, that our culture—let me stress this—and our religious traditions were ingrained with such feeling long before the fifties came along. All of us, whether we admit it or not, are in some measure shaped by this cultural inheritance, and this inheritance cannot be overturned in a day."

Quite a speech. He would keep it short and snappy next time.

No one spoke. Andrews tried to gather himself. He had been up since five in the morning when Kate had roused him from the effects of the sleeping pill he had taken at midnight. The actual flight time was short, but he had to change planes and there had been a long wait. The glass of wine he had drunk to show the committee he was not a legalist was making him sleepy. He felt himself sucked deeper into the bog. He would try one last time.

"What I'm saying is that if a church where I was pastor voted to adopt an open and affirming policy, I would do my best to support it. I would do so in good faith, believing that the policy was right. But if that policy resulted in the church becoming—well—a kind of Mecca for gays and lesbians, given my background, I might not be the best person to play host."

There was a throaty laugh, so loud that the people at the next table turned around. Andrews looked up to see Patti Leone grinning at him. "That's the truest thing," she said, "I've heard anybody say since this committee started meeting back in the days before the flood."

As if by pre-arrangement, the questioning ceased and people fell seriously to eating. Andrews had a chance to study them. He had come to like Jim Purdy over the telephone, and now that they'd met, Andrews liked him even more. He was a tall, spare man in his middle-sixties, with thin, sandy hair, and a face that looked as if he spent much time outdoors. Purdy's was an open face, yet wise and assured, the face of a man on whom others had come to rely. On the way from the motel to the restaurant, Jim said that over the last thirty-five years he had served on just about every board and committee in the church, presided at pancake breakfasts, acquired land for a parking lot, persuaded the organist not to bring sexual harassment charges against the bass soloist, and remained on reasonably good terms with four senior pastors and their associates, some of whom were "pretty odd ducks."

"As far as I can tell," Jim said, "I don't represent any faction, so they made me chairman, or, should I say, chairperson. I should have known better than to take the job on."

He chuckled.

"A lot of work?" Jack asked.

"A lot of work and a lot of pressure."

Andrews could tell that had he felt it appropriate, Jim could have gone into a good deal of detail about the pressure part.

As dessert was served, Jim reviewed for everyone present the coming schedule of events. After dinner, he would take Reverend Andrews back to the motel. At nine the following morning, Harry and Mark would pick him up for a complete tour of the church premises. At ten-thirty, Reverend Andrews would meet with the interim senior minister, Dr. Purnell. At noon, Paul would come by the church and take Jack to lunch at the University Club. Anyone else on the committee would be welcome to join them. Paul would also show Jack the highlights of the campus. Jim would meet them in front of the library at two o'clock and, as time allowed, would run their guest through one or two residential neighborhoods so that he could get an idea of the housing situation. Jim felt this was important, especially since Reverend Andrews lived in a parsonage currently, and Epiphany did not own a residence. At four o'clock sharp, the whole committee would convene with the candidate in the fireside room at the church. This would be followed by a buffet supper at Purdy's, and hopefully Jack would be back to the motel by nine for a good night's rest. On Sunday, of course, he would be preaching in Ulverston at ten a.m., and if anyone was uncertain how to get there, maps would be available at tomorrow's supper.

When Jim had finished, Patti Leone grinned again. "It's called the 'Epiphany Endurance Run,'" she said. "We've killed off three clergy already that way. Think you can survive it, Pastor?"

He suspected his smile was wan. "I'll try."

Jim pushed back his chair. "Anybody have any questions?"

Andrews heard his own voice. "I just wanted to confirm that I'll be meeting with the interim pastor."

"I'm glad you brought that up," Jim told him. "I know it isn't usually done at this point. In fact, Dr. Clayburgh was against it. But we felt it would be a way for the candi . . . for you . . . to ask some questions about the church of someone knowledgeable who's not a member and can be objective."

"Dr. Purnell has done a wonderful job here," Hilda said. "He's helped with a lot of healing."

"That's right," Jim agreed. "But we want it to be clear that Dr. Purnell will not be interviewing you with the idea that he's going to make a recommendation to the committee. We agreed with Dr. Clayburgh, the denominational man, that would not be right at all—"

"In fact," Paul Knudson cut in, "we haven't asked Dr. Purnell to report on any of the candidates. The purpose of your meeting with him is simply to help you obtain a more complete picture of the church from a fellow professional."

"I understand," Andrews said.

"All right then," Jim said, and pushed back his chair all the way.

Andrews glanced at the brass label below one of the

gilt-edged photographs on the wall of the restaurant. It read "J. Henley Brooks, 'Whiskers,' English Lit., 1932-1948."

The photograph shed no light on the origin of the sobriquet:  J. Henley Brooks was clean-shaven.

# CHAPTER SEVEN

Andrews had trouble believing that Thomas Chalmers Purnell was real. Dr. Purnell brought to mind those old Calvert Whiskey ads. All the man needed was a glass of amber liquid held with elegant inevitability in his right hand and a Great Dane stretched at his feet. "The Man of Distinction." But someone had said Dr. Purnell was a teetotaler and that he even preached a sermon on temperance to tittering in the choir. Otherwise, it was said, the interim minister was highly respected.

Purnell's head was tilted toward the light, which played softly on his bronzed hair. Was it natural? Andrews had researched the man's date of ordination. Purnell had to be well over sixty.

"I'm glad they gave us this opportunity to chat," Purnell

said. His apparent distinction did not lie in symmetrical good looks. The ridges over his eyes would have seemed prehistoric in a face less elevated. His massive jaw was worthy of C. Aubrey Smith.

"I'm glad, too," Andrews said. "You recently retired, I believe, from Colby Memorial in Cleveland."

"Shaker Heights," Purnell corrected him. "Yes." He sighed heavily. "Yes, I retired somewhat early. My wife and I hope to do some traveling, and I have a book or two in mind."

Andrews now remembered where he had seen Purnell's distinguished face before. It graced the dust jacket of a book he had picked up at a meeting somewhere. The title first attracted him: *Modern Man and the Christian Imperative*. But as Andrews stood at the book table skimming through the pages, he found the text vague and platitudinous, one of those popular manifestos in which Christianity was boiled down to two or three harmless and unexceptional sentiments.

Purnell leaned back farther in the upholstered swivel chair he had rolled out from behind the desk. He crossed his legs. "What can I tell you about Epiphany Church?"

Andrews felt ashamed at not having given their meeting much thought. "Well," he began, "you might share your impression about the morale of the church, how they've reacted to the departure of Norman Goodens."

Purnell smiled. "I'm not sure 'departure' is the right word. Norman and his wife have chosen to retire locally and have moved into an apartment on the other side of town. Of course they attend another church, but he's still around."

"Oh?"

"I don't want to give the wrong impression," the interim minister said quickly. "It's not as if he is interfering especially. When he retired, he announced that he would not perform any weddings or funerals here, and I think he means it. But I keep running into him at people's houses."

"I see." Andrews supposed that the possibility should have occurred to him. But no one on the committee had said anything about Goodens still being on the scene.

"It happens a lot these days," Purnell said. "We used to be taught that ministerial ethics demanded withdrawal from the community when one retired—at least for a time. That's one reason I decided to take an interim a long way off. But the old rules are eroding."

Despite the suspicious color of his hair, Purnell sounded sincere.

"Well, I suppose I shouldn't be surprised," Andrews said. "Goodens was here a long time. It's hard to let go."

"Right. And as I said, I think he has let go in most ways. One thing he's done, however, is to promote one of his friends to be his successor."

"Really?"

"Yes. But I don't think you need to worry about competition from that quarter. The committee did look into him. Goodens is highly respected here, and they felt they owed it to him to follow up on his recommendation. The man's out in St. Louis, I believe. In a big church there. But I gather that after reading his résumé, the committee decided not to pursue him. They're a pretty independent lot, as you may have noticed, and when some of the older members, prompted by Goodens, began putting the pressure on, the committee rebelled."

"How did Goodens react to that?"

"I don't know. Naturally, I haven't asked him." His great jaw rose. "You need to understand that I don't mix into the activities of the search committee. That would not be appropriate. I only know about this because Jim Purdy was so distressed by the matter that he came to talk to me about it."

Purnell looked as if he feared that he may have said too much.

Andrews began again, "Well, the matter of Norman Goodens aside, Dr. Purnell—"

The hand that might have held the Calvert's Whiskey rose in protest. "Please. Call me Tom."

"Okay, Tom. Aside from this business about Norman Goodens and his friend, would you say the church was in fairly healthy shape?"

"Oh, I'd say so. Of course whenever a senior pastor leaves, you have to expect all the demons to come popping out."

"How do you mean?" Andrews hoped his alarm did not show.

"Well, a lot of little personality conflicts, competing factions, that sort of thing. But that's only natural. I wouldn't say it was a big problem here."

Andrews did not want to let the subject drop. "Exactly what are the factions competing over?"

Purnell pursed his lips, assumed a judicious frown. "Well, there's the open and affirming thing, of course, and there's some dissatisfaction over the Sunday school. Mostly, I think it's tension between the old guard, a lot of them retired faculty, and the younger people."

"I gather the church has been aging on the whole."

"That's right. But there are some very active young families who were brought in by Kempel, the former associate minister. Some of them were upset that he felt he had to leave when Goodens did."

Purnell must have seen some discomfort in Andrews' eyes because he threw out his hands in a kind of pulpit gesture, smiled widely, and said, "But all that is minor stuff. I've been here ten months and I really think the church is over the hump and ready to rally under new leadership."

"I'm sure," Andrews told him, "that they've profited from the kind of experienced leadership you've been able to give them. People on the committee have told me how grateful they are to you."

Even Purnell's shrug was elegant. "What can I say? It's been a blessing to be here, though my wife and I look forward to the interim ending soon. We don't even have a home of our own, you know. We agreed to come here before I'd even finished up at Shaker's Heights." Another heavy sigh. He looked away, toward the shrubs outside the window. "A number of people here have suggested that I might stay at Epiphany for a few years as the regular pastor." He fixed his gaze on Andrews. "But, of course, I couldn't do that, could I?"

99

"No, I suppose not."

"No." Purnell sighed again. "The rules may be eroding, but if I broke that one, I'd never be asked to do another interim." He laughed. "Not that I'd want to. I'd be too old."

At first Andrews found it exhilarating to sit in the comfort of the fireside room as the center of attention. Fielding the committee's questions, he prided himself on dissecting each one systematically.

"You're asking three things, I think. First, as to whether children should be involved in the Sunday worship, then the matter of Sunday school curriculum, and finally parental participation. Let me begin by saying . . ."

But Andrews soon grew weary. To be truthful, exhausted. He wasn't sure what he was saying half the time. He was trying to become more clipped in his answers. He checked his watch. Almost time to break before supper at Purdy's home.

"Reverend Andrews?"

Last night, the boy hadn't said a word. Nor earlier in the afternoon when Andrews had expected a question about his senior high program at New Sharon. It wasn't much of a program. Two or three kids might show up on a Sunday afternoon. But the youth had done one thing recently that seemed significant. They had put on a play about Jonah that Andrews had written. All day Andrews had been looking for an opening to talk about the play.

"Matt?"

"Reverend Andrews, I was reading an article, I think it

was in *Time*, which we get for social studies, about a clergyman leaving the ministry. It said there were quite a few
these days, and I wondered if you'd considered doing that."

"You mean maybe the churches would be better off if I
did?"

The whole committee laughed.

Matt blushed. "No. I just wondered if you ever thought
about it."

Laughter was good, but not at the boy's expense. Matt's
question was one that Andrews had not anticipated. He
would need to be more deliberate in answering. He would
need to watch his compulsive candor.

"I wouldn't be normal if I hadn't thought about it, Matt.
It's a demanding and sometimes heartbreaking profession.
But somehow I've never been able to imagine myself doing
anything else."

The boy was still interested. "Have any of your friends
quit the ministry?" he asked.

"Well, yes. Back in the late sixties and early seventies,
those were hard times, several people I knew left the ministry. I had a friend who was my roommate during my first
year at theological school. He was a Barthian, a follower of
the Swiss theologian, Karl Barth, which I won't try to go
into, except to say that it made him more orthodox than me.
For my friend, 'liberal' was a dirty word even then. In religion, not in politics. In politics he's always been a liberal.
We had a lot of arguments. He was a very brilliant fellow.
He went into the ministry of the Presbyterian Church, and
then, in the late sixties, during the furor over Vietnam, I

101

heard he'd left the church entirely. I wrote to him, asking whether what I'd heard was true, and he wrote back: 'I'm one of those rats leaving the sinking ship.'"

Andrews could hear Hilda catch her breath.

"So what did he do then?" Matt asked.

Andrews looked around the room. They were behind schedule now, but he could tell that people were interested in hearing more of the story. "Well, Matt, for a time he tried to support himself—I should add that he was also divorced during this period—by selling a new line of biodegradable cosmetics and cleaning products. I ordered some floor cleaner from him, for our church floors. It didn't work very well."

Laughter again.

"Then I lost track of him. Imagine my surprise when, two years after the floor cleaner incident, I ran into my friend while vacationing in New England. He told me he was now minister of a large Unitarian church near Boston. He was full of enthusiasm for his congregation and his work. His church was looking for a co-pastor, and he suggested I apply. 'We'd make a good team,' he told me."

Hilda Cox cut in. "And what did you tell him?"

"I said that I respected the Unitarians for their questing spirit and dedication to high ideals, but that there was something ineradicably Christian about me. And so we argued about that. My friend claimed his theology was still more Christian than mine. But the point is that, though he changed denominations in a rather radical way, in the end he found he could not leave the ministry."

The boy seemed satisfied. The questioning ended. At least for a time.

The church in Ulverston consisted of a pale stucco building with a square tower, high stone steps, and pointed windows that rose behind a stand of sugar maples about fifteen miles down the same highway as the motel. Andrews gazed through the windshield of Curtiss Myrick's Buick as they waited in a small parking lot. The old lawyer had appeared at the motel early to pick Andrews up. They had arrived at their destination by twenty after nine. Even at that hour, Andrews hoped that the church would be open so that he could "case the chancel," as he put it jokingly. He would have welcomed, too, a few minutes alone when he could read through the service and his sermon manuscript one more time.

But the church was locked. The pastor, Andrews learned later, had grasped the opportunity afforded by a guest preacher to spend the weekend at his brother-in-law's lake cottage. The custodian didn't work on Sundays, and no one else, it turned out, had been assigned to open the doors.

"I'm supposed to be the reactionary on the committee," the lawyer said. "They put me on to balance people like Knudson and the Leone woman. Actually, I regard myself as a progressive."

"I see."

"It's just that I'm sick and tired," Myrick went on, "of these denominational conventions passing half-cocked resolutions on everything from alimony to plastic bags. Most of these people have no practical understanding of what they're shouting about."

"Possibly not."

"In my view, the church ought to concentrate on a few key issues of clear and overwhelming moral significance."

"I've sometimes felt that way."

Just then a little blue Ford pulled up beside the Buick. A small middle-aged woman got out and looked at them.

"Is the church open?" she asked.

"All the doors appear to be locked," Myrick informed her.

"Well, they told me where to find a key."

Andrews and Myrick followed the woman as she went up the stone steps at the front of the church and ran her hand along the molding above one of the doors.

"Here it is."

Though the key slid into the lock and turned the tumblers, the heavy door would not open. Andrews took hold of the marble knob and pulled so hard that if Myrick hadn't caught him, he would have fallen backwards down the steps. But the door did open.

"You the guest minister?" the woman asked.

"Yes."

"I'm the substitute organist, and this is my first time here." She started down an aisle in search of her instrument.

Andrews found a light switch and looked around. The space inside was a familiar adaptation of a turn-of-the-century style of Protestant interior known as "The Akron Plan." A heavy oak pulpit stood on a raised platform in front of three large chairs upholstered in black leather. Behind the chairs rose a choir loft, flanked by tiers of organ pipes painted gold. Andrews suspected that the biggest pipes were dummies. The pulpit and choir loft faced several rows of curved pews, also made of oak, and arranged in semi-circular fashion on a sloping floor.

Leaving Myrick in one of the pews, Andrews passed through a sliding partition in search of the pastor's study. He found it rather quickly, a dark room with a large desk and a small bookshelf. There was a slip of paper on the desk with "Welcome" typed on it, followed by a request that prayers be offered for someone undergoing hip surgery in the community hospital. Two copies of the Sunday bulletin lay nearby. Andrews flipped though one to make sure the order of service was the same as he had received. Then he snapped open his attaché case and lifted out his sermon.

A shriek, then a sustained cry so loud and so high that it actually produced pain. He covered his ears with his hands. The sound persisted. He got up and, still covering his ears, ran into the sanctuary. There he found the substitute organist screaming at the lawyer.

"I can't stop it," she cried. "It just keeps going, no matter what I do."

Andrews decided afterwards that only Providence could have directed him so quickly to the ladder that led to the organ loft. He scrambled up the rungs, Myrick told people later, like a squirrel pursued by a cat. There was a trap door at the top of the ladder, which he knocked open with a violent thrust of his head. Once he had hoisted himself into the loft, he had no trouble locating the offending pipe. Quickly he pulled the pipe loose. The shriek was replaced by a menacing hiss. That would give the organ a wheeze, he told himself, but it was nothing compared to that piercing howl.

Worshippers were beginning to arrive when Andrews climbed down. He recognized Patti Leone, who waved to him, and young Matt. Self-conscious, Andrews saw that his suit was covered with dust. But Myrick came forward beaming. It was a rare thing for a minister, the old lawyer said, to be a man of action.

Back in the study, Andrews checked his watch. Go minus four minutes. The organist had already begun to play her prelude. No time to go over the service. Quickly, he unzipped his garment bag and pulled out his pulpit robe. He had taken pains to hang the bag in his motel room, but Myrick had stuffed it into the Buick's trunk, and the robe was badly wrinkled again. Andrews hoped some of the creases would fall out as he walked around. Finding no mirror in the study, he ran into the men's room and tried to correct what his venture into the organ loft had done to his hair. He looked at his watch again. Ten o'clock exactly. He stood for an instant by the urinal and prayed. He was ready.

Below the pulpit lay a dozen rows of golden oak, all empty. Somewhere in the distance curved the long final pews. There, a handful of worshippers crouched, their faces shadowed by the overhang of the empty balcony. Despite the dimness, it was not hard for Andrews to pick out the Epiphany committee. Most of the locals were elderly, though there were two or three young adults with children. During the opening prayer, a baby began to cry and continued relentlessly until halfway through the sermon. At that point—Andrews thought of it as the climactic moment in his message—the mother stood up and, climbing over a series of extended knees, bore her child into the narthex. All heads turned in her direction as the baby was carried out of sight, though not entirely out of hearing.

Long before this incident, Andrews felt himself giving way to a spirit of fatalism. He barely looked at his manuscript. He let the text carry him. It was a text that had carried him much of his life: *For by grace you have been saved through faith. And this is not your own doing, it is a gift of God.*

Following the service, Andrews stood at the top of the stone steps, the skirt of his robe billowing in the breeze. Few of the faces that passed appeared glad for his presence, not even the face of the woman in the flowered hat who said his sermon gave her "food for thought." The one enthusiast was a white-bearded man with a cane.

"I hope they choose you," the man said, his tone conspiratorial.

So they knew why he was there.

Another face now, another hand. He thought he remembered the woman's face from the time of the doxology. She was sitting in the back pew, and something about her drew his attention. Maybe it was the way her chin lifted.

"Hello, Jack."

"Laurel?" He heard his voice speak her name before his

eyes recognized her.

"It's me. I hope you don't mind. I heard that you were coming."

The woman was Laurel, though she looked much older and out of shape.

"Of course I don't mind. Nice to see you—"

Someone else in line appeared eager to shake his hand or to pass by him. Laurel stepped back into the obscurity of the narthex. When the last worshipper trailed down the steps, Andrews knew that he would have to go back inside the church. He had to remove his robe, recover his papers from the pulpit, and take a look at himself in the men's room mirror. Perhaps Laurel would not be inside. Perhaps he had not seen her at all.

She was there, standing beside the display case that held the memorial book. He started to move toward her when Jim Purdy approached.

"Hello, Laurel," Jim said. His voice was cordial. "Have you met Jack Andrews?"

She came out of the shadows a little. "Yes," she said. "Years ago, in fact."

"Oh. Well, then, I'll just leave you two to talk over old times while I catch one or two of my committee before they get away." He looked at Andrews. "Then I'll be back to take you to lunch before we head to the airport."

As Jim ran down the steps, Andrews moved closer to Laurel. "So you know Jim Purdy," he said.

"Yes. I worked for him a while back. He's a nice man."

"He is. What are you doing now?"

"Selling real estate. I have my own little business here in Ulverston."

"You've left the ministry then?"

Her smile was cryptic. "I never really got started."

"You mean after Foster? You never went to another church?"

"When they reassigned me, I withdrew. I was never ordained."

He felt a burden of sadness descend. "I'm sorry," he said.

She shrugged. "I'm not. I found other things to do with my life."

He wondered what. But not very hard. His mind did not want to go that way. He was relieved when he heard Jim calling to him from the bottom of the steps.

"You'd better go along," Laurel said. When she smiled, her eyes were still the same.

"Yes," he said, "I guess I'd better."


On the way back into the city, Jim apologized for having chosen such an unpromising place for Andrews to preach.

"We didn't know what it was like," he said. "We thought it was a larger congregation and that they'd be a little better organized."

"I'm sure it's hard to plan these things."

"It is, especially when, as I'm sure you know, we've had to schedule several of these situations for our candidates. It's a time of year when ministers are reluctant to give up their pulpits. Things are starting again after the summer slow-down. But we should have looked into Ulverston more carefully. Still," Jim turned and smiled, "you proved that you can meet the challenge."

"I hope so."

"Believe me, you did."

They drove in silence for a few minutes when Jim asked, "Known Laurel Haynes a long time, have you?"

"I knew her for a short time a long time ago. She served a little Methodist church when I was in Iowa."

"Foster?" Jim had read Andrews' ministerial dossier carefully.

"That's right. After seminary in the East, I was called to be assistant pastor in a big church in the Chicago suburbs. But after a couple of years, I decided I wanted a church of my own, so I went to this little place in Iowa called Foster."

"I think I went through there once," Jim said. "Nice little town."

"Yes, it is. And it was a nice little church. I still have a lot of feeling for the place. Kate always liked it. Our two children were born there. Sometimes I'm sorry I moved on as soon as I did."

"I'm sure your talents called for a larger field of service," Jim said.

"Maybe. Anyway, after we'd been there a couple of years, Laurel came to serve a Methodist congregation even smaller than mine. She was still finishing her work on her theological degree."

"Had some trouble, she told me once."

"Yes. It was one of those congregations dominated by

one extended family, a kind of clan. All the clan tensions came out in the church. The lay leader told the bishop that they'd welcome a woman pastor, which was the last thing the clan was looking for."

"Maybe he thought he could order a woman around," Jim said.

"Maybe." Andrews recalled how he had met that lay leader on the street one day and the man had gone into a long complaint about how unsuited Laurel was for the ministry. Some smoldering fire of chivalry flamed up in Andrews then, and, though he hardly knew the woman, he had risen angrily to her defense. He still marvelled when he recalled the incident. He was always such a gentle soul in those days. But he had lit into the man so stridently that one of his own officers came in to talk to him about it. The Methodist leader, after all, was president of the Kiwanis.

"Laurel worked for me awhile," Jim said. "I felt sorry for her. She seemed like someone who had missed the boat, if you know what I mean. But she got her brokerage license and moved out here to Ulverston. I understand that she's doing real well."

Andrews knew how easy it was to feel sorry for Laurel. Sympathy was the lever by which she moved him. He was chairman of the clergy association in Foster when Laurel began attending meetings. She was still a student at a seminary some distance away, and, at first, she only came to Foster on weekends. But soon she made special trips to attend the midweek clergy events. One evening she hosted the meeting in the half-furnished parsonage her church provided her. After the meeting was over, she asked Andrews if she could speak privately with him. He stayed and listened and sympathized.

After that, Laurel consulted Andrews quite frequently. She was as old as he, possibly older. But she told him that she considered him to be her mentor in the ministry. No one else she knew was so gifted or so understanding of her situation. Without these opportunities to talk with him, she doubted she could survive another week at that "den of robbers" to which the bishop had assigned her.

Andrews supposed he was flattered. He encouraged their conferences, whether at his church or in the tiny Methodist parsonage. He always came away feeling that he had been of some use.

It was after a week in which her church board had treated her especially carelessly that Laurel asked Andrews to drop by for a moment. As soon as she opened the door, she broke out crying. His first impulse was to run away. Tears made him uncomfortable in those days. Instead, he began patting her shoulder. She clung to him. Before he knew it, things were getting out of hand. She went to her bedroom to find a handkerchief and blow her nose. Andrews waited in the living room. When he heard her crying again, he went to find her.

A year or so later, it occurred to Andrews that Laurel was more intentional and more experienced than he had realized at the time.

Jim was talking again. "I guess she wasn't at that church in Foster very long, from what she told me."

"No." To tell the truth, and it was a truth in which he had taken refuge long ago, he was glad, truly glad when the bishop announced he had other plans for Laurel Haynes. "No," he said again, "she didn't stay very long. Only a month or so, as I recall."

Hardly any time at all, compared to the twenty-odd years Andrews had spent forgetting. Still, that one instant. Timeless. How much he had underrated what the ancients called concupiscence. His pride had led him to believe that it was only the sin of pride that mattered in the end, that pride alone could be a man's undoing. How ironic it was that the flesh could lift his spirit so. That instant when she exploded around him, he passed beyond himself. Going in unto her. So deeply. Was that what Meister Eckhardt meant by the divine abyss? Was he touching God at last?

Jim Purdy stood watching as Andrews passed through the security check. Hoisting his garment bag, the minister turned quickly and waved. He then picked up his small bag and walked quickly down the long aisle, slowly diminishing in the distance.

A good man, Jim thought. He could tell that Andrews had impressed just about everyone on the committee. A week ago it seemed that they would only be going through the motions with Andrews. They had invited him, so they had to interview him and hear him preach. Before Andrews arrived, the decision was between Kevin Belton and Maria

Shilling. The fourth finalist turned out to be a total bust. Funny how different a man could be in person from the way he appeared on paper. But both Belton and Shilling had a lot going for them. Both were young, in their late thirties, and both had a record of heading strong youth programs as associate ministers in large churches. And both gave the impression they were up to date on everything in the church.

The impression left Jim feeling ill at ease with them, especially with Belton. He knew that most of the committee thought that Belton was nearly ideal for Epiphany. Not quite as intellectual, perhaps, as someone like Paul Knudson might wish, but in tune with many members of the congregation. There was no fear that Belton would say something wrong; he knew the right words for everything. Dr. Clayburgh and the other denominational people advising the search committee saw Belton as a young man of great promise.

But Jim wasn't so sure. He didn't know how to express his doubts, even to himself, but it seemed to him that everything about Belton was on the surface. He had not imagined the day when he would come to this, but he actually preferred the young woman. She was not only personable, but she was sharp. She would make a good senior pastor. He was tired of all the "-ing" words certain church people used these days: caring, nurturing, empowering. And he was weary of those "-nesses": wholeness, oneness. The words seemed to turn everything into the consistency of one-minute oatmeal. Maria Shilling would lead the congregation without all that mush. Jim had heard her preach twice, once in her present church, where he went to visit with Paul, and once locally at a neutral pulpit. And he had to admit the lady delivered a damn good sermon.

The trouble was Harry Bauman, who always did have a way of throwing air balls when the score was tied. He made the comment that if the church hired a woman, some people would leave. And, of course, that set off Patti Leone. If Patti appreciated Belton before Bauman's comment, she would stand in concrete for Shilling after. And probably Sue Grant would do the same, though she was more quiet about it.

The committee had agreed at the start that no candidate would be recommended to the congregation unless he or she received the support of at least two-thirds of the committee. At this point, that understanding could lead to a deadlock. And given the bad feelings over the way Bauman raised the issue of a woman pastor, they might have to disband the committee and ask the church board to appoint a new one. Because they had spent ten months at the task already, that would be a real waste. Dr. Clayburgh, the denominational man, didn't seem to feel starting over would do much harm. But Jim knew that wasn't so. People were tired of waiting.

And then came Andrews. Admittedly he was fifty-eight. He had spent most of his time in small towns. In fact, after Andrews went back to the motel last night, Paul Knudson made the comment that despite a residue of "preppiness," there was a "touch of hayseed" in Andrews. Well, that was all right with Jim Purdy; he came from the boondocks himself. Epiphany could use someone who was down to earth, as long as he could still push ideas around with the professor types. And it was clear that Andrews could do that. Maybe Knudson was afraid of him.

Andrews wasn't Mr. Congeniality. Not a glad hand and a big "ho-ho." Some people expected those qualities in a minister, though this was less the case at Epiphany than at most places. Jim visualized Andrews again as they sat in the fireside room the day before. It was hot—no need for a fire—and the man looked exhausted. At one point, Jim feared Andrews was ill, his face was so drawn and pale. But he kept answering the committee's questions. Everything from zero-based budgeting to liberation theology, even Sunday school attendance pins. Sometimes he seemed a little uncertain what to say. But he never ducked anything and he never gave a pat answer. He wrestled with the questions in a way that Belton, for example, never did. Jim had the feeling that Andrews was a man who wrestled with questions all the time.

Jim told himself that Andrews might be just the pastor Epiphany needed right now. If he could give them six or seven good years, that would be fine. After Norman Goodens' long pastorate, they needed a period of transition. A young minister who came in with a lot of new ideas and ran roughshod over everything Goodens had set up would find himself in trouble from the start. Not that Belton or Shilling were likely to do that. Belton was too smooth, and Shilling, too sensitive. Even so, either choice would strike the congregation as different from what they had known. Andrews was more like Goodens. He came from the same generation, and his worship style was more traditional. He had experience, even if most of it was in little towns.

As he walked out to the airport parking lot, Jim was still mulling the candidates over. He had more or less written Andrews off before this weekend, but now he was beginning to feel that the man from New Sharon might be the answer to their problems. He reminded himself that he should drive to Ulverston and talk with Laurel Haynes. Take her out to lunch, see how she was doing, and get her impressions of Andrews. Evidently it was a long time since she had known anything about this work, but a personal reaction from somebody outside the committee might prove helpful.

It was anybody's bet how the committee would decide now. Jim remembered somewhere in the Bible when they were choosing one of the kings. A man looks on the outward appearance of a candidate, but God looks on the heart. Well, God knew nobody on the committee had divine vision. How did anyone see past the facade and all the dry facts in a résumé? Jim dreaded the next meeting. He thought he'd propose that the first ten minutes be spent in silent prayer.

# CHAPTER EIGHT

On the way back from the cemetery, the talk was freer and more spirited. It was almost as if the minister were not there in the front seat. Or perhaps the pallbearers now accepted him in a different way, as someone who, having divested himself of death's dignity, might be treated like anyone else. Still, Andrews found himself on the outside because the talk centered on reminiscences he did not share. Ancient history was the theme, and, whenever memories came into conflict, the funeral director was drawn in as the court of appeal. Old Greene knew more secrets about New Sharon's citizens than the bartender at the Triangle Tavern, more financial information than the loan officer at The Farmers and Merchants Bank, more family lineage than the resident genealogist, more local lore than the president of the historical society.

"Christ, Frank," exclaimed one of the voices, "didn't Homer Plank have a place over on the West Road where he ran a still back in the thirties?"

"Naw. That wasn't Plank. That was Howard Miller."

"But I thought Miller lived over on the creek."

"He did. That's where the still was. Right, Ted?"

"Right," Old Greene answered. "The still was on the creek, but it belonged to Homer Plank."

"Okay," the voice said. "I got it straight now. And the grandson lives in town. What's his name? Jerold?"

"Garrold," Old Greene said.

"Yeah. Garrold. Garrold Plank. Wasn't he in the Air Force?"

"He got out years ago," Frank said. "He works for Delmo Advertising."

The sepulchral voice wanted to know if Johnson still owned the business.

"He sold out," Frank told him.

"Who to?"

"Somebody from out of town. You've seen him. He's in Kiwanis. Higgins, ain't it? That's it. Higgins."

"Hoskins," Old Greene corrected. "Henry Hoskins."

"And Johnson retired to Florida, didn't he, Ted?"

"Fort Myers," Old Greene said. "We buried him in Forest Hill last May."

There was a brief break in the conversation as the limousine came to a stop behind a truck making a turn into a gravel pit. Delay, Andrews had decided long ago, was the order of the day. The fates had conspired to postpone things. Which was all right, since his hope, after all, was against odds.

Frank must have continued thinking about Delmo Advertising, because as soon as the limousine began to pick up speed he recalled the receptionist at Delmo when Johnson owned the company. "Remember that bleached blonde?"

"They're all bleached blondes these days," another voice said.

"Yeah, but this one was there maybe fifteen years ago. They said she invited clients home for dinner at fifty dollars a plate."

"I remember hearing that," the backseat voice confirmed. "You hear that, Ted?"

"Something like that," Old Greene said. "Can't believe everything you hear."

"That's true. But could be Frank was what you call an eyewitness."

Frank laughed. "Don't let the Reverend hear. He might tell my pastor."

The other man leaned forward. "You wouldn't do that, would you, Reverend? You don't talk to Lutherans, do you?"

"Not if I can help it," Andrews said.

"See, Frank. You've got nothing to fear. I did hear, though, that Dick Cole was involved with that blonde. They say the hunting accident that did him in wasn't exactly accidental."

"I guess I heard those rumors," Frank said. "Know anything about that, Ted?"

"I'd say that if it drops five degrees tonight, it could snow," Old Greene said.

Andrews had been drifting off again, recalling every word said during his inquisition in the Epiphany Church fireside room. He woke from his reverie to see the outskirts of New Sharon. Home. Yet never quite. Always pilgrim and exile.

A hasty October twilight was passing over the town as he looked down from Gordon's Hill. The street lights were on, as were the headlights of approaching cars. Yet there was still enough radiance in the sky to reveal the profiles of the buildings. In another twenty minutes their separate identities would merge into dark. At this moment, though, he could make out the square tower of his church. It rose above heavy oaks, his fixed mark in this and other passings.

Further along, the limousine crossed the intersection where, less than three hours earlier, the accident had taken place. If any signs of the event remained, none could be seen. The place knew it no more.

"You fellows all want to go straight on to the funeral home," Old Greene asked, "or shall I drop you off at the Ramsey house?"

"Might as well take me to the Ramseys'," one of the pallbearers answered. "My wife should be there. She's got the car."

"You can drop me at the Ramseys', too," Andrews said,

"it's only a short walk for me from there."

He spoke without thinking about the letter. If he had asked Greene to take him to the church, he might have read the letter sooner. He had interposed something else. How was this possible? Why was he so perverse? There was still time. He could change his mind. But the limousine was pulling up in front of Myra Ramsey's home. He might as well get out with the others.

The door was opened by one of the Ramsey daughters. She reached for Andrews' coat. "That was a nice service, Reverend," she said, "I enjoyed it very much."

He watched her hang his heavy overcoat in the closet by the front door. "Thank you, Jane. How are things in Neenah these days?"

Her smile revealed surprise. "You have a good memory," she said, "seeing as I don't get home much and, when I do, I'm afraid it's rare I make it to church."

"Oh, but your mother talks about you. And I think I recall seeing you at last year's Christmas bazaar."

"Was I there?"

"I think so."

She shook her head as if to shake the cobwebs loose. "I guess you're right," she said.

She pointed him toward the dining room where he could see that the feast was already in full sway. All the extra leaves had been added to the table to accommodate the dishes brought in by neighbors and Myra's circle at the church. Spread out on Myra's best linen cloth was a variety of casseroles, salads, cakes, and cookies.

"Take all you want, Reverend Andrews," Jane told him. "People brought so much over I don't know what we're going to do with it all." She left him and returned to the front hallway.

He wondered if Kate remembered to go light on dinner tonight. And that he would be late.

Ginny Schultz, a member of his flock, sat at one end of the table as official pourer. She was in her late sixties, a chain-smoker with a deep voice. Reputed to be the richest widow in town, she was descended from the first settler of New Sharon, Jeremy Wells, and had been married to a lawyer from Cleveland who came to own half the business district. After his death she had twice cruised around the world, and she continued to chair a committee that arranged an annual bus trip to the opera in Chicago. She might have functioned as the town's grand dame were it not that there was a touch of the ribald about Ginny that diminished her authority.

"Hey, Jack," she called, "be sure to try that meatball dish. Ingrid made it, and it's the real thing."

Jack obeyed promptly, though limiting his portion of the meatballs to one serving spoon. He knew Ingrid's cooking was good, but what would Kate say?

"I want to congratulate you," Ginny said.

"What for?"

"For not reading that bit about many mansions. I get sick of it."

"Oh, well . . ."

"I bet you get sick of it, too, Jack. And the Twenty-third

Psalm."

"Well, maybe."

She laughed. "You bet you do. You can't kid me. Take some more of those meatballs. They'll get you through the night."

He took another small serving and moved on to the potato salad. This time he sampled less than a spoonful.

"Oh, you can do better than that, Reverend."

He looked over his shoulder to see Myra Ramsey, his hostess.

"Well, I'd like to, Myra, but when I get home my wife will have prepared dinner and . . ."

"Oh, I'm sure you can handle it, Reverend."

He hoped so. Perhaps Kate had the foresight not to prepare dinner at all. But that was unlikely. Somehow she never understood about these affairs. And when she heard all the things he had eaten, she would be annoyed. He need not tell her, of course, but she would know. She always did.

He moved slowly into the family room with the immense picture window. He remembered looking out at the bank of white trillium that led down to the creek. It was one of those many times he coveted his neighbor's house. It was a natural envy. He had never owned a home of his own. The parsonage was a fairly comfortable house, but it was not his choice. Given the power to choose, he would not have opted to live next to the church. And had he chosen, he would have found a place with a view like that from this room. Of course, it was dark out there now, and the trillium would not return until spring. But the creek was there, and the woods, to look out on every morning.

Searching for a place to sit, he slipped into a folding chair in a small opening between somebody's uncle and a sleepy young woman in a black velvet skirt that kept riding up her thigh. He tried to look someplace else, but, cramped as he was in a narrow space, there were not many options. Not that the young woman seemed to mind if people looked at her. He was tempted to reach over and pull her skirt down to cover her knees.

The mood of Mr. Upsall's mourners was not so jolly as an Irish wake—no alcohol was served—but that pervasive good feeling was back again. It hung among them like a pink mist. Mrs. Ramsey was laughing as her brother described the time they all got stuck in a snow drift. "And Mother walked home by herself two miles in the storm, she was so mad. She said Dad should have known better than to drive without chains."

"She was a great lady," somebody's uncle said. A thin-faced man with narrow shoulders and a large pot belly, his odd proportions troubled Andrews as might a faulty syllogism.

"Dad never was the same after she passed away," Mrs. Ramsey said. "They were married fifty-four years. He was never the same, you know."

A darkness in the mist then. A blue cloud of pathos that loomed above them like a blimp and then blew off with a burst of laughter from the next room.

Andrews looked around. There were a lot of people whom he had never seen before. Every so often Myra

Ramsey brought one over to be introduced. There was a grandson from Arizona and a grandniece from the Upper Peninsula. There was a baby brother, aged eighty-eight from the Masonic home in Lenox, and there was a great-grandson who was going to Yale. Andrews sensed that these people hardly knew one another, if indeed, they had ever met at all. Yet all were flushed now with delight in their common bond. Even the son's colleagues from Harper Wire and Cable were connected. Blood was thick, but death was thicker still, and in its pasty flow all of them cohered.

For that hour.

Somebody's uncle waddled into the dining room, changing places with the great grandson going to Yale. He was tall and thin with dense black eyebrows above his glasses, and he struck Andrews as one of those young men whose every gesture toward persons older than himself exuded condescension. Yet there was a quality of naive curiosity about him that at times submerged his arrogance. He peered at the girl in the velvet skirt without much interest and then turned to face the minister.

"Do you go to many of these things?" he asked.

"A few."

"All in a day's work then."

"Some days," Andrews said. "I only do about a dozen funerals a year. And not all of them involve gatherings like this."

The young man looked surprised. "I thought that you people spent most of your time doing weddings and funerals."

"That's probably because you only see people like me at weddings and funerals," Andrews said.

"Touché." The Yale man coughed. "I was wondering what your theory is about the decline of the mainline church."

Andrews pursed his lips. "I have a different theory every day," he said.

The Yale man raised his dense eyebrows. "You admit there's been a decline."

"Yes. No doubt about that."

"You mean in numbers?"

"In numbers. But also in other ways."

"Such as what?" the Yale man asked.

Andrews thought for a moment. "In influence, for one thing. In confidence, for another. In clarity and unity of purpose, for a third. In a sense of definite identity and community. That's four at least. I could go on, but I think that's enough for now."

"I surprised to hear you admit all this," the young man said. "Most ministers I know—not that I've known many— but they always seem to be saying everything is just okay."

Andrews nodded. "I know. That's the way you get when you're the front man for an institution. And the truth is, the decline took a lot of us by surprise. After World War II, it looked as if we were going to be favored by an endless religious boom."

"I have a professor—" the Yale man said. He was sitting on a folding lounge chair, and he leaned back now contentedly. "I have a professor—he teaches sociology—he says that what's really involved here is a crisis in WASP culture. Would you agree with that?"

"By 'WASP culture,' your professor is evidently referring to people whose religious heritage lies in those churches that were dominant in early America. They were mainly British in origin, but their membership today is certainly more diverse."

The Yale man sat up and uncrossed his legs, crooking them so that they dangled from either side of the chaise lounge. "Okay," he said, "let's not quibble over words. We both know whom we mean. You admit these churches have been declining. This professor I'm talking about says that religion reinforces people's social identity—or, at least, it's supposed to. That's mainly what it's for. I mean, for example, the black churches foster black pride. And various immigrant groups, like the Italians or Poles or what have you, found in their churches a place where they could remember who they were and celebrate that. But the WASP—sorry, but this professor does use the word—the 'early American' churches, don't do that for their people anymore. Instead, they make people feel guilty about who they are. Their preachers are always putting them down for putting down all the other groups. It's the latest form of the Puritan conscience breaking out, this professor says. Only now, it's a kind of group self-disgust. Everybody else blames the WASPs for everything that's wrong, even in places where they're a small minority, this professor says, and these preachers just play into it."

"Is this professor WASP?" Andrews asked.

The young man thought for a moment. "Well, I guess so. At least, he seems the type."

"Like you."

The Yale man actually grinned. "Like me. Anyway, this professor says that the WASPs are the one group in America who can't celebrate who they are—at least, not in church. So their churches are dying. And beyond that, he sees a general decay in WASP culture . . ."

"It's not a bad theory," Andrews said. "It could be argued that it's precisely the guilt you speak of that keeps people from protesting the use of the term, 'WASP', which keeps appearing in the press. But I can think of ways in which the theory doesn't work so well."

"Oh? What ways?"

"Well, for one thing, the most 'Anglo-Saxon' religious groups around are probably Evangelical ones emanating from the South. And they are growing. What your professor is describing is something that's been going on in the more liberal denominations, centered in the North."

The young man nodded. Some of his condescension had fallen away. "That's a good point," he said. "But what's your latest theory? You say you have a different one every day."

Andrews laughed. "Oh, the latest one is the loss of hell."

The fellow appeared puzzled. "I don't know what you mean."

"Well, for some time now, the people in the kinds of churches you have in mind have pretty much forgotten about hell. If you took an opinion poll, some might say they still believe in it, but they don't worry about it much. For most liberal Christians, hell is an un-Christian notion. But there was a time when people in these churches took it very seriously and that gave going to church a certain urgency, if you see what I mean."

"You mean, fear," the young man said. "Fear of hell made people go to church."

"Yes. But not only fear. Compassion, too. Fear motivates people to want to stay out of hell, but compassion—charity—moves them to want to keep other people out. Hell kept the missionaries going, the evangelists. And it gave the church authority, made it authoritarian, in fact. You might say that so long as belief in hell prevails, the church is in a perpetual state of martial law."

The young man's brow furrowed. "So you're saying, without hell it's hard to keep people excited about church?"

"Right. Nothing the denominational task forces have been able to come up with quite replaces hell in that regard."

The young man actually laughed. "But I've heard people say—like my mother, for example—that hell is a state of mind. Or it's things people experience here in this life, like poverty, oppression."

Andrews nodded. "I know. People say those things. But you see, they are not really talking about hell. Hell means retribution, a just punishment. A person may do a very evil thing and afterwards enjoy a happy state of mind, which is certainly not just. Oppression, by definition, leads to unjust suffering. And, terrible though it may be, unjust suffering is not truly hell. On the contrary, it makes people long for the comfort of hell."

"Now you've got me confused," the young man admitted.

It had been months since Andrews enjoyed such a good time. Even his discussion with the Epiphany search committee in their fireside room was not this stimulating. He had to be cautious then. "Well, you see, people are comforted by the faith that, in the end, evil gets its comeuppance. Without that faith, it's hard to make sense of life. It's the longing for retributive justice, to use a fancy name for it. Come to think of it, this may be one reason people are so strong on the death penalty right now. It's a feeble gesture toward replacing the loss of hell."

"I'm not sure I understand," the Yale man said.

Andrews tried again. "In a world like this," he answered slowly, "people want to believe that in the end everyone receives his or her just desserts. Obviously that doesn't happen in life. Most people still believe in heaven, but heaven makes for a lopsided universe. You might say that without hell, heaven is amoral. You need hell—or, at the very least, some sort of purgatory—to give people the sense that there is a moral order to things. But when hell falls out of favor—as it has in churches like mine these days—well, the church can't offer that sense of moral order to people."

The Yale man's eyes looked a little glazed. "You surprise me," he said. "I took you for the God-is-love type."

"I am."

"But now you bring hell in."

"I know. But you asked me for my latest theory on why the liberal mainline Protestant churches are declining. I've given you today's theory. I wouldn't place too much stock in this one." Andrews stood up. "I've got to be getting home," he said, and picking up his empty plate, he began to move away.

"But what about you?" the young man called after him.

Andrews turned.

"But what about you? Do you believe in hell?"

"Hell knows," the minister said, and headed for the kitchen.

Picking his way through the crowd, Andrews bumped into Jason Higgins.

"Hello, Reverend," Jason said, "did you hear Ellen and me are back together?"

Andrews said that he had heard. He did not add that he found the news surprising. Jason and Ellen had come to talk with him once when they were on the verge of separating. The interview had ended in a major row. Shortly afterwards they had separated. In fact, Andrews had been told that Ellen was filing for divorce. He could not say he blamed her.

"I'm glad," he told Jason, "that you've been able to work things out."

"Oh, I wouldn't say we worked things out, Reverend—just stuffed everything under the rug."

Jason swayed forward, and for an instant Andrews felt himself in danger of going under from the power of the man's breath. Alcohol might not have been served officially at the wake, but there were those who had apparently managed to bootleg it in.

"You know, women are like dogs," Jason said.

"No, I didn't know that." He always thought of dogs as male, even the female ones.

"They're always watching you," Jason said. "They even read your mind. You ever had a dog, Reverend?"

"Yes." He hadn't owned a dog for many years and knew his neighbor, Mrs. Shook, wouldn't like it if he did. The parsonage yard was too small in any case.

"Well," said Jason, "if you ever had a dog, you know what I mean." He listed sideways as he spoke. "If you get the idea in your head that you want to take him for a walk, he comes running before you make a move."

"As Albert Payson Terhune used to say," Andrews told him, "dogs are uncanny."

Jason straightened himself for an instant. "Albert who?"

"Terhune. He wrote stories about dogs. I used to like them when I was a boy."

"Yeah. Well, I bet Terhoozy didn't know beans about women. You had a dog, you say. You got a wife, right?"

"Right."

"Well then, you know what I mean."

Jason reeled forward and disappeared into the crowd. Andrews made his way to the vestibule where the Ramseys were saying their farewells.

"Did you get enough to eat?" Mrs. Ramsey asked Andrews.

"Yes. Thank you."

"I'm so glad," she said, "that boy wasn't hurt bad. I mean the one whose truck was in the accident."

"Yes, that's what I heard—just bruises." He had overheard people talking about it when he came in.

"Sure fouled up the procession, though," Mrs. Ramsey said. "Sometimes I think they ought to raise the driving age to thirty-five." She then told her husband to get the minister's coat.

"I saw you talking to Gerry's boy, Reverend," she said. "He goes to Yale, you know. Gerry wanted him to go to the university like the rest of the children, but Clark got a scholarship to Yale, and I guess he's suited for it."

"I guess so. We had a very interesting conversation."

Mrs. Ramsey leaned forward and whispered in his ear. "I saw you with Jason Higgins. Isn't it nice that he and Ellen are back together?"

He didn't need to answer. Bill Ramsey was helping him stuff his arms into his overcoat, and his face was forced toward the floor. With his coat on, Andrews said, "It was nice to see Jane again."

Myra Ramsey looked pleased. "She was so happy that you remembered her. I don't know how you do it."

"Oh, I guess it's because you speak about her so often. I don't remember everybody."

It was true. Sometimes Andrews forgot the names of people he saw every week. They were so anonymous, passing through the door on Sundays.

"Well, we appreciate all you've done," Myra Ramsey said. "We know Dad wasn't a church-goer, but he enjoyed that call you made so much."

"I enjoyed it, too." And as he thought about it, he really had.

"It was a nice service," Bill Ramsey told him. "Short and to the point."

People in New Sharon always said that about Andrews' funerals. And yet he wondered what other ministers did at funerals that took so long. He really didn't know. He'd only attended two or three funerals as a mourner.

Walking into the dark, Andrews felt the sense of elation still clinging to him. It had been a good day, he thought. He had been useful, part of things, less of a stranger.

It wasn't until he reached the corner that he remembered again about the letter.

# CHAPTER NINE

Andrews' heavy coat was more than a match for the dying wind. Hatless, he felt his ears begin to tingle. But that was all right; the cold would help clear his brain. It was only four blocks down Parsons Avenue to the Gothic tower. He almost wished his walk might be longer.

He thought again how absurd it was that he should care about moving. Why was he subjecting himself to needless stress? Why did he put himself again into a situation where he was hounded by an unrealistic hope? If by some miracle his hope were fulfilled, the situation would probably turn out to be a disappointment. Like many old saws, the one about life and hope worked both ways: where there's hope, there's life. Hope kept you breathing. For Andrews, applying for pastoral openings was like buying lottery tickets. So long as his name was under consideration, life was full of possibilities.

But why was he not content to stay in New Sharon? No answer that he might come up with was likely to square with a call to selfless service. Well, why hadn't Paul stayed in Tarsus? Or Troas? Or Philippi? But then no voice in the night had cried out to John Mason Andrews, "Come over and help us!" John Mason Andrews was not commissioned to be an apostle. He was supposed to be a settled pastor. Why then couldn't he settle?

Ambition was part of the answer, or it had been once. Ambition was not something talked about in the ministry. To be considered ambitious could be as deadly for a minister as for Julius Caesar. But that didn't make it any less a factor. Several moves back, he had told himself that it was best to face up honestly to the force of ambition and to grant that force a measure of satisfaction. Otherwise, you fell prey to hypocrisy and, depending on how your ambitions worked out, you either feigned saintly disinterest in your good fortune or played the martyr. He'd encountered both mind-sets in countless clergy, and they were not attractive. You couldn't repress ambition anymore than you could repress sex without growing morbid in some way. So, he once asked himself, why not harness ambition, let it drive you on to genuine achievement in the service of the Lord? He suspected now that his line of reasoning was a shameless bit of casuistry, but he had taken pride in it at the time. He had seen it, in fact, as an example of what the great theologian, Reinhold Niebuhr, called, "Christian realism."

But what could ambition mean for the parish ministry? Where did it lead? In a non-hierarchial denomination such as his own, he could not aspire to a purple vest. The days were past when leading preachers were household names whose sermons were reported in the metropolitan dailies. Come to think of it, he could name five or six men who were preaching on Fifth Avenue when he was born. But he couldn't name anyone who was preaching there today or anywhere comparable. The only famous preachers were those huckstering TV evangelists who appalled him as grotesque caricatures of everything the church and its ministry meant to him.

He supposed success for someone like him meant a large congregation, preferably a wealthy one, or one that contained influential people. At least, that was what it had meant a few years earlier. Fewer influential people seemed to go to church these days, and what was a large congregation today would have seemed barely a step from an entry level pastorate when he had entered the ministry. Relative size and influence still counted, though.

And a multiple staff. You had not arrived in the eyes of your colleagues unless you had at least one ordained person working under you. That was still a reasonable goal, because a modest-sized church might have more than one minister these days. It was another paradox of the times reflected in institutions outside the church. Smaller memberships, fewer activities, but more staff. Not in New Sharon, though. There wasn't enough money.

But did he care about all that? No doubt there were many

ways to understand success in the ministry. What troubled him was that the ideals driving him were not truly his own. They were derivative, based on the values of others. Every field imposes on the individual a crass standard of professional worth. But the imposition was harder to bear in the ministry because of the nearly universal denial that such a standard existed. You were not supposed to "play the numbers game" or act as if attendance and budget figures had anything to do with your success as a pastor. You were not even to think of such a profane notion as "success" in connection with yourself. When you were in touch with one of the denominational placement people about seeking something larger, they gave you the feeling that you were saying something a little off-color. Yet you knew damn well that they rated you and your church, however unconsciously, in terms of how much you sent into the denominational coffers—"the Mission." You knew damn well, too, that they paid a lot more attention to the pastors of big churches. You knew all of that, and goddamn well. And he could say that, because he wasn't blaspheming, he was only speaking God's mind on the whole business.

Yet he knew that what really counted with him were not these collegial pressures. It was parental expectations. His parents were dead, long dead. They had been not much older than he was now when they died. If they were still alive, as they well might have been, they would have been disappointed that he had not amounted to something more. Granted, his father was not enthusiastic about his going into the ministry. Still, since he did go in, why could he not have done something like his father's classmate, Zeke Van Arsdale, who had that big church in Farmington, Connecticut, and wrote that bestselling book—what was it?

Something more was expected. No matter how independent you thought you were, you were always being directed by the judgments of other people. He supposed that even the attitudes of his old school and college friends had something to do with how the force of ambition played out in him. Anymore, he only heard from two or three of these men, and then only in notes on Christmas cards written by their wives. He doubted that they, or others he had known in the distant past, ever thought about his career at all. But suppose they did? Suppose they had followed his career? The question ought not to matter, but it did. He was bullied by the hypothetical. He had sensed long ago that, for most of the people he had known early in life, his going into the ministry was strange in itself. That was not hypothetical; that was a fact. For him to have spent thirty-odd years running mimeographs in little midwestern towns had to be something quite beyond their comprehension. They might have approved an authentic sacrifice, especially one that was widely celebrated. They might have accepted him in an Albert Schweitzer role. But what he had been doing all these years would have seemed to them demeaning, shabby, even self-destructive in his individual case, if, in a more general way, admirable.

But, surely, it never occurred to any of those people to think about what he was doing, so why did it matter? He had gone his own way. He had made his own choices based on his own preferences. He would not want to be back there in that New England suburb going to pot. He liked small towns where everyone was somebody. He liked the familiarity, the intimacy, even the gossip and endemic conflict. He liked to be able to drive out into the countryside on an impulse to watch the ducks land in spring pools beside fields of new rye so green it pained the eye, or to startle at a burst of crows rising from the stubble of cut corn, their cries rousing passions in him that had no name.

Why should he bow to the expectations of the long dead? He hoped he had not foisted a similar burden of expectation on his own children. He had to admit he was pleased Bill had won a full-tuition scholarship to Colgate. He couldn't have afforded to send his son to a place like that otherwise. He had never pressured Bill to go to a good Eastern school, but he had to admit he was pleased. He knew that, had they been alive, his own parents would have been pleased, too. Andrews would always pride himself on going his own way, and he wanted his children to do the same. Yet, experience had won from him the grudging admission that one never escaped the expectations of others. You might wrestle with them like Jacob with the angel. Come dawn, you might even think you had bested them. But they kept coming back. He doubted anybody would ever accomplish very much without the expectations of others. More than once he had preached a sermon on the notion that God's expectation goads human beings to live up to their destinies. Sometimes he thought the whole Bible could be interpreted in the light of that idea.

So what did all that mean with regard to his seeking another church? Were there no expectations still to be fulfilled in New Sharon? Had he nothing more to offer in that place? Sometimes, like a cold hand clapped against his heart, the thought came to him that he had nothing more to offer anywhere. He was like the Saul from whom the Spirit had departed. And all around him were young Davids strumming their harps, singing all the current tunes, and, despite their pious protestations, quite willing that he be cut down by the Philistines.

Yet he did have the experience for something larger and more challenging. He could say that honestly and in all modesty. He had paid his dues. And in order to do his best he needed something more intellectually and institutionally stimulating. Except for the dinners and fund-raisers, he had never been able to interest the New Sharon church in much more than the weekly service and the children's Sunday School. Not that he didn't keep busy. It was not uncommon for him to drive fifty miles to visit someone in the hospital. Almost every week he sat over the fried chicken waiting to give the benediction at some community event. He spent an average of twenty hours or more weekly just preparing his sermons and services. Still, there was something lacking in the quality of his experience that he believed a place like Epiphany might fill. People had ideas there, and social concern, and a sensitivity to the arts—that tremendous statue of Hosea in the atrium!

Kate was right. If he stayed much longer in New Sharon he would rot. On the other hand, at a place like Epiphany, he would blossom, rise to new heights of wisdom and eloquence, recover his vanishing faith, become something more than he had ever been before.

He laughed out loud. Right there on the street. Pride goeth before. But it was possible. What Kate didn't admit was something he had learned in his travels: in fundamental ways, the Epiphanies of this world are not much different from the New Sharons. Still, she was right. Holy Spirit aside, a prestigious pulpit would fire up his self-esteem. And he would become a better minister. Pride goeth to a strange variety of destinations.

When he entered the ministry, he had taken for granted that he would end up as senior minister of a large and sophisticated congregation. It did not seem a prideful expectation. The expectation was shared by most of his seminary classmates. A good many other ministers around served promising congregations without appearing to have much on the ball. Lightweights, most of them. Bland. Men who substituted sentimentality for the gospel, the kind who baptized babies with rosebuds. A tougher, sharper, more prophetic generation ground by the mills of depression and war was coming along to replace those false prophets. Then watch the Church revive!

It was clear that many like himself had taken too much for granted. The churches were still growing then, even in liberal denominations such as his own. They were not growing as fast as they should have been, considering the baby boom. But the mood was euphoric until finally even the denominational bureaucrats began to acknowledge that the statistics were turning the other way. Whatever its causes, the Yale man's professor was right about the decline. Some of those churches that rose up so dramatically in the new suburbs after World War II were now only shadows of their former selves. The churches in the old suburbs like the one he grew up in were faring even worse. They lived off their endowments. The big city churches had suffered most of all. It was, he believed, the New Sharon-type churches that were holding up best. His congregation had kept pretty much on the same level since he had been there. There were three hundred and thirty-six confirmed members and an average Sunday attendance of one hundred and seventeen. Both figures were above average for his denomination. And though the program wasn't what he might have wished, there were quite a few activities. At least his church wasn't a mere adjunct to a daycare center.

So why then should he want to move? Because over the last thirty years he had gone through a succession of little places where he did everything from setting up the banquet tables to replacing the float valves in the toilets. Over the years, after much waiting, some churches had come his way. Once he had reached the final four for a senior pastorship of one of the most prestigious churches in the country. He never knew who had put his name in, but hearing from that church out of the blue lifted his spirits to unprecedented heights. Just flying in for the interview was like leading a triumphal procession. The committee treated him royally. They put him up in the best hotel in town, dined him at a country club reputed to have one of the eight best golf courses in the world. Afterwards, their chairman wrote a personal letter stating what a powerful impression Andrews had made. But they called someone else. Andrews heard him speak once at a conference on spirituality, a plump little man with the sheen of a keynote speaker at a sales convention.

All this happened shortly before Andrews came to New Sharon. Sometimes he thought of his interview at that prestigious church as the high point of his career. It was like shooting for the basket from the far end of the court just before the final buzzer and having the ball circle the rim before popping out again. Depressing in the long run, but for a second or two, stupendous.

He supposed that if he had been more active in denominational affairs, served on more committees, attended more meetings, he might have had more chances. Those kinds of things counted with the denominational executives who made recommendations. The trouble was that he was always so far away from where meetings were held, and, as time went on, he found them tiresome and unproductive. He felt he was better employed at home.

His mind was divided. The truth was that he liked setting up banquet tables. It was one of the ways he got some exercise. And he was proud of the current tables, which he had ordered himself. As for the float valves, they represented one of the very few skills he had acquired in the course of his labors as a pastor. When replacing a float valve, he felt as if he rated the title "Artisan": a man who put things together, who righted a specific wrong. His father couldn't have done it. He doubted that Dr. Longworth could have done it either.

And he cherished every bit of glass in those windows that looked like a thousand other windows in a thousand other churches—Jesus knocking at the door, Jesus blessing the little children. And he cherished the dark tower he could see from almost every point in town and toward which he looked daily for reassurance. When he woke up one morning to find that lightning had knocked off one of the tower's little concrete points, he burst into tears. To his surprise, Hank Pearson, chair of the trustees, had confessed the same reaction. Good man, Hank, as good a man as might be found anywhere. Inside of two weeks, the tower had been repaired.

If he left New Sharon, there would be grief. But that was inevitable. Living in time (and live he must) meant perpetual grieving. Every moment was a losing. And a gaining. If one had the right outlook, the next moment could bring the quality of wonder. Grief and wonder. What else was there?

The dark brick tower of midwestern Gothic was only a block away now. He picked up his pace. He would meet his moment of reckoning.

But someone was approaching.

# CHAPTER TEN

"Say, Reverend, if you're headed for the church, I got something to give you." It was Harley Berry who confronted Andrews from across the street. "I seen you going by, Reverend, and I thought I'd just hand you these pledge cards seeing as you're headed toward the church."

In September, the chairman of the church finance committee had suggested that they hold their pledge drive earlier than in the past. It was traditional to observe Stewardship Sunday around the second or third week of November. But, increasingly, other organizations were finding that a productive time of year for fund-raising, and so were competing with the church's effort. The chairman's proposal was that the church move up its campaign to the middle of

October. Andrews encouraged the experiment, partly because of the interest that Epiphany Church was showing in him. It was not egotism to believe that his resignation at New Sharon after so many years might have an unsettling effect on the church. To resign during the pledge drive might prove disastrous.

For some years, his church had abandoned the traditional membership canvass for a direct-mail approach. Only those who failed to send in their pledges by a given Sunday received a personal call. One problem with the technique was that it tended to demoralize the people charged with making the calls. Enthusiastic members usually made a point of getting their pledges in on time. The people on the calling lists were likely to be those who were either indifferent or dissatisfied. The reports of the personal visits also tended to demoralize the minister.

Andrews took the cards from Harley and put them in his pocket. "I'll see the financial secretary gets them," he said. He made it a practice not to know what people's pledges were.

"There's a couple of notes attached that you'll want to read," Harley told him. "The Dokers are moving to California, so naturally they don't want to pledge."

"Oh, I didn't know that."

"Yep. Well, I guess Bill is retiring, and they want to be nearer their daughter out there. And then there's the climate."

"Do you know when they're leaving? I'd like to drop by before they go."

Harley took off his hat, scratched his head, then put the hat back on at a slightly different angle. He said, "I don't think they're actually planning to move until next summer."

Or maybe not until the next canvass, Andrews thought.

"There are a couple of other things," Harley said. He hesitated. "The Meyers are unhappy."

Andrews felt a knotting sensation in his gut.

"Oh, what about?"

"Well, it seems, Reverend, that Mr. Meyer is put out because you didn't call on his sister when she was ill."

"I didn't know she was ill." The sister had moved back to New Sharon recently, and he had called on her once to invite her to church. She hadn't seemed very interested. "Nobody told me about her," he added. "Is she still sick? What was her trouble?"

"I don't know what her trouble was," Harley said. "I guess she's okay now from what Mr. Meyer told me. So far as I know, she never went to the hospital. It's just that they think you should've called."

"I see."

"And then there's the Plochs."

"The Plochs?"

Harley pulled his hat down tighter about his ears. "Getting cold," he said. "The Plochs say they're transferring to a church in Kane City because you want to bring blacks in here."

"You mean into the church?"

"I guess so," Harley said.

"But how could I do that? There aren't any blacks within

a radius of thirty miles."

Harley shook his head and smiled. "I don't know, Reverend. But that's what they said. They said you was always talking about how our churches were too segregated, and, before we know it, you'll have us full of blacks like that church on the other side of Madison."

"It's the craziest thing I've ever heard. That church they have in mind is in a largely black neighborhood." Andrews could tell his voice was growing shrill, so he lowered his tone a little. "Even if I tried, there's no way I could fill our church with African Americans."

Harley smiled again. "I know," he said. "I told the Plochs that. I guess it's just that they think you would do it if you could."

Andrews wanted to say that the Plochs were good riddance. But as with many things he wanted to say, he swallowed the wish. Instead, he said quietly, "Well, since the Plochs know me so well, I guess they'll be happier in Kane City."

"I hope so, Reverend. But it's hard losing good givers like that."

So, he would take the blame again.

As Harley went back across the street, Andrews walked on slowly. His mood was turning. The opinions of the Plochs or the Meyers or the Dokers may not strike someone else as mattering much, but such things accumulate over time. They added up to the end of joy. And it was always his fault. No matter how unfair. He was ready to move on. He wouldn't stay in New Sharon a day longer if he could help it.

Under the circumstances, it was reasonable to feel more than slightly annoyed with God. The feeling wasn't new. It wasn't long ago that he had succumbed to a kind of cosmic outrage. After he had returned from meeting with the Epiphany people and delivering his candidating sermon, much time had gone by when he didn't hear anything. If nothing else, the silence was discourteous. Actually it lasted less than three weeks, but it had seemed much longer. He was all but certain that he had been eliminated. He became depressed. And angry. He nearly concluded that, as the Catholics were fond of putting it, he had lost his faith. He had observed more than once that when people lost faith in themselves, they were most likely to lose faith in God. His faith in himself was at rock bottom. But that insight came to him later, after better news. At the time, he said of his faith what he wanted to say about the Plochs: good riddance!

It was right at his low point that Ruth Carlson came to see him. She had recently been through a nasty divorce from a man who kept exposing himself on street corners. Try living with that in a small town! And her sister was dying of cancer at the age of thirty-nine. Add to that, the house Ruth was renting caught fire because of faulty wiring. Most of her things and those of her two children were lost. She had a lawyer, and she expected to get something back from the landlord's insurance as well as her own. But that wasn't the point. It was the trauma, the loss of keepsakes, the feeling that everything was turning against her.

She began to weep. After a time she said quietly, "It's not fair! I'm no saint, but I always thought I was a reasonably good person."

"You always seemed that kind of person to me," Andrews told her reassuringly.

"Then if there really is a Higher Power, why am I treated this way?"

He had never cared much for the expression "Higher Power." It was a phrase a friend of his parents had kept repeating after he joined Alcoholics Anonymous. Andrews discovered later that the term was given currency in "The Big Book." He supposed that, in context, it served a good purpose. Many alcoholics were brow-beaten by traditional religious language. But Higher Power struck him as vague and slippery, smelling of the sick dependency he associated with another saying popular in certain circles when he was young: "Let go, let God." It was a favorite of his mother's, her advice for any unhappy occasion. *Let go, let God.* It angered him when his mother said it, especially when she said it to him. It seemed like a cop-out, to use an expression of later currency.

But he couldn't bother Ruth Carlson with his biases about religious language. He could only say that he didn't know why fate seemed to be picking on her, but that the Power was there and that it was with her.

Afterwards he wondered if he had been honest. How did he know? He felt he had been treated pretty unfairly himself. What troubled him lately was not the notion that God was the antidote to human impotence—nor even the belief that there was a Higher Power—but the suspicion that the Power had gone awry.

Back in his theological school days, Andrews had come up with his own abstraction. In a small discussion group, he had said that Christianity was, in a nutshell, a belief in the unity of power and goodness. He didn't know where the idea came from; he doubted it could be original, but the thought impressed the teaching assistant leading his group. For weeks they strayed from the textbook to work over that summary formula. *The unity of power and goodness.* Though Andrews was not initially aware that he had done so, he had put into words an ultimate optimism. Good had to win. In the end, power had to be benign. Power without goodness, the teaching assistant had declared, could not be divine. At least, it was not consistent with the biblical picture of God, and in that school, liberal though it was, a concept that was not biblical was clearly out of bounds.

Then it occurred to Andrews to pose a question: "What of goodness without power?"

The teaching assistant rejected that possibility, too. Not only was it not biblical, it was not even possible. For how could an entity be good without the power to be good? Andrews did not try to answer that question. However, he wondered if, to be good, God's power had to be unlimited. Before he could raise that issue, someone brought up the matter of babies born with water on the brain.

Nothing was resolved about the babies. Not that Andrews expected anything would be. Long ago, he reminded himself, he had learned to live with the problem of evil. You took that for granted. It was a primary datum— like death. If you had faith, it was in spite of or not at all.

But Andrews had asked another question. Might God be all-powerful, omnipotent, but not entirely good? Or maybe, not infinitely powerful either? Just considerably powerful and considerably good? The teaching assistant professed to find these questions too obscure. He had grown impatient with Andrews. It was possible, he said, to get bogged down in abstractions. What mattered was the Cross, the sweat on Jesus' brow, the spear in his side.

Andrews agreed. He still agreed. The older he got, the less he bothered about theology at all. Religion was concrete or it was nothing. It was action. It was passion. It was symbol. But he was afflicted periodically with that abstract turn of mind. And every so often his inspired thought returned: the faith to which he was committed was the unity of power and goodness. At the heart of everything. Fundamental optimism kept Christianity going. Not a shallow optimism, but one in spite of the Cross, and paradoxically, one because of the Cross. Because the Cross was the goodness that had to win. The unity of power and goodness. He couldn't prove it. He had to take it or leave it. For more than thirty years, his life and his work were predicated on his taking it. Yet, lately, he was tempted to leave it. Not because of any new questions or answers, but because some balance within himself had tipped the other way. He almost blurted out that he thought Ruth Carlson should leave it, too.

The odd thing was that he still believed in God. For God never had been a grand abstraction to him. God was something *there*—like the trees. But this thinking about how God was *there* was undergoing a radical change. He began to think of God not as the Higher Power but as the Supreme Bumbler—well-meaning, but a kind of ultimate poor dumb slob.

There was something greater than ourselves. Andrews never doubted that. There was something that hurt even more than we do, and was confused even more than we are. Something that called for our pity like the drunks he used to see on Sunday mornings on his way to his seminary field-work assignment—men, and occasionally women, puking on the subway platform. God was like them. Of course, such a God called for our revulsion, too—our disgust. Most modern men who gave up on religion did so out of disgust. But a God infinitely pathetic might move us beyond disgust, beyond pity even, toward compassion. For God was well-meaning. And so, by our compassion for the Supreme Bumbler, we might be saved.

Once or twice it occurred to Andrews that "The Supreme Bumbler" might make an interesting sermon. So far he had resisted the temptation. Not that yielding to it would have gotten him burned at the stake. The people in his congregation would simply have yawned and said to him afterwards at the door, "Enjoyed your sermon, Reverend." Even at a place like Epiphany, they probably would have done that.

A few days later, his thoughts following Ruth Carlson's visit struck Andrews as crazy. But there it was. It would remain part of him like all his other sins. And having reconstructed his conception of God, he had gone to work on himself. If God was the Supreme Bumbler, he, John Mason Andrews, M. Div., was a true disciple. He was a bumbler of a lesser sort. He had been a bumbler all his life, and that business with Laurel was a prime case in point.

Meeting her again had thrown him into a panic. And what an irony the timing was! Right there at his candidating sermon! Perhaps he should add to his conception of God the notion of Supreme Joker. Again and again in his experience, the idea seemed to fit. But running into Laurel after so many years had upset him for several reasons. He thought that he had buried Laurel—laid her to rest in a concrete vault. And here she was resurrected, alive.

Flying home from his weekend with the Epiphany search committee, Andrews reflected that his brief affair with Laurel Haynes was an event on the same order as the organ cipher that came close to destroying his candidating sermon. Both events belonged to the crazy and unpredictable. They were irruptions of the surd into the good order of his life. He could not prevent either from happening, but he did manage to put a stop to both of them.

But his latest attempt to explain the affair never made it as far as the landing strip. Laurel and the organ pipe might have some features in common. Both took him by surprise. Trapped by his own good intentions, his own pity for Laurel's troubles, he was struck down by sex. But there was one decisive difference. He was not responsible for the organ cipher. He was responsible for what happened with Laurel.

Andrews had broken off the affair even before Laurel

was transferred out of Foster. He did not believe that anyone other than he and Laurel knew of their relationship. The affair ended so quickly that it was easy to imagine that it never had happened. But Andrews knew from the start that damage was done. Damage was done to Laurel. It was true that she had "come on" to him. But she also had come to him seeking help, and he had violated her trust. He doubted that Laurel's life was the better for the relationship. He had been only twenty-nine at the time, and had he been older and more experienced, he might not have been caught off guard. But he was old enough to know better.

He had damaged Kate, too. An outsider might assume that there had been something seriously wrong with his marriage. Andrews did not believe there was. He always loved Kate. He never loved her any less because of his affair with Laurel. He loved himself a lot less, though. He discovered the wisdom in those biblical interpreters who stressed the last two words of the commandment "love thy neighbor as thyself." Without the right sort of self-love, you couldn't love anybody as you should, not even your wife. Laurel did not make him love Kate any less, but his loss of self-respect got in the way of his love.

It got in the way of his loving God, too. At the outset of his ministry, Andrews disciplined himself to set aside a half hour every morning for prayer and meditation. After his encounter with Laurel, he found he could not get through those half hours. His devotional discipline never fully returned.

Brief though it may have been, Andrews' affair with

Laurel opened a great wound of self-doubt in the center of his psyche. The event humbled him. As time went on, he put up fences around himself. He would not call on a woman alone. He would not see a woman in his study at night unless someone else was in the building. Such rules might have amused his colleagues as something out of a Victorian handbook on the parish ministry. Andrews did not care. The Victorians were right about some things.

By the grace of God, Andrews believed that he had forgiven himself, put the matter behind him. There was a saying he had employed more than once in sermons: "Let the past be past." It was a catchy, simplistic slogan that one of the positive-thinking preachers might have invented. Andrews was a little ashamed of himself for promoting such a saying. But he believed sincerely that many people's lives were blighted by the mistakes of their past. There came a time when, as Paul put it, one had to forget what lies behind. Let the past be past. The saying caught on with people, and Andrews believed that it accomplished some good.

But the past never remained entirely past. Not with the Supreme Joker at work. Andrews would like to believe that almost thirty years ago, he had done something wrong and repented and that was that. But the incident in his past defied simple classification. He would like to dismiss the incident as merely sordid, but that description did not do it justice. His thought about touching the divine abyss wasn't entirely self-mockery. Something wondrous entered his moments with Laurel. There was a glory in them that no measure of guilt or cynicism could deny. And whenever he brought the glory to mind, the wound of self-doubt grew wider. Life was too complex for belief. After Laurel, nothing was certain.

Since running into Laurel again, Andrews had begun to worry that Jim Purdy would get the idea of talking to her about him. He had no reason to believe that Laurel harbored any ill will toward him. She had seemed cordial enough that day. After all, she had gone out of her way to hear him preach. But he did not know her anymore. The truth was that he never had known her very well. He certainly did not know what to expect from her after all this time. A legacy of distrust clung to him, not concerning her goodwill but her judgment. He worried that if she said anything to Jim Purdy at all, it would come out wrong. And Purdy was shrewd. He picked up on things.

Then that letter came in the small, square envelope that stood out from the rest of the mail with a pinkish tan that was close to the typical complexion of the people lying in state at T. C. Greene & Son. The note paper inside was the same color and was alive with the scent of gardenias. The message was handwritten:

*Dear Jack,*

*I wanted to let you know that Jim Purdy came by yesterday and asked me about you. I told him that I was in Foster, Iowa, only a short time, but that you had the reputation of being the best all-round minister in town.*

*Here's hoping you get the job. If you do, you may be assured that I'll keep out of sight.*

*Laurel*

Her note was reassuring if only because it showed that Jim Purdy was still interested in Andrews. He wasn't sure what the words revealed about Laurel.

A few days later, a letter came from Jim Purdy, saying that the committee was taking longer than expected to come to a decision, but implying that he was still in the running. For some reason, Millie had put the letter on his desk rather than in his pigeon-hole, and when he saw it there, all the anxiety and all the anger streamed out of him. Nothing but despair remained. He knew the rule of late years: positive news travels by telephone; rejections go out in the mail. Despite this knowledge, he tore open the envelope immediately: *Just a note to let you know we haven't forgotten you . . . taking a little longer than anticipated . . .*

Purdy's message offered a glimmer of hope. Andrews had proved more than a résumé, a "pastoral profile"; his personal presence had made some impression. The Supreme Bumbler might have stumbled over a bit of kindly providence. The possibility sent Andrews home whistling that evening.

Later, he worried that Purdy's letter meant the committee had deadlocked, forcing them to put aside all the present candidates and to move on to a new group of finalists. For the delay to go on much longer would not be a good sign.

He wondered if he should respond to the letter. Clearly, Jim was writing to keep him on the hook, to forestall his accepting a call somewhere else while the Epiphany committee pondered its choice. No doubt, letters had gone out to all the remaining candidates. Since a reply wasn't asked for, Andrews decided not to send one. He would not seem too eager. He would keep them guessing.

Another couple of weeks went by before the latest letter arrived. It could be quite inconsequential. It might simply contain some information about the church. Andrews recalled that a committee member had promised to send him a list of topics the adult forum was taking up. He would come to no conclusions about the letter in advance.

Andrews stood beneath the Gothic tower. The illuminated bulletin confronted him with the topic for Sunday's sermon: *The Cost of Discipleship*. Credit Bonhoeffer with the title. It was a retread of something Andrews had preached long ago. He found lately that he lacked the inspiration to come up with new ideas. Even so, he was never satisfied with something he had done in the past. Reworking the old one was taking longer than most sermons he started from scratch. He'd spent one whole morning coming up with a new beginning. The ending was not yet in sight.

He headed for the smaller of two front doors, the one to the side of the high stone steps, which led most directly to the church office. There were lights on inside. One was on the basement level, probably the ladies' room. That light was always left on. Another light shone through the colored windows of the nave, or the sanctuary as it was known in churches like his. What could anyone be doing in there?

He took out his key chain. There were so many keys on it that he was thinking of wearing suspenders. Lately, his belt had a way of sagging below his paunch. The door open, his right hand fumbled for the light switch at the foot of the stairs. He froze for an instant as a terrifying sound ripped through the ecclesiastical darkness. The telephone was ringing.

# CHAPTER ELEVEN

"Pastor Andrews?" The strong intonation of the voice was distinctly southern.

"Speaking."

"Pastor, this is Gaylord Partridge calling long distance from Nothnagle, Texas."

Was it possible that his name was circulating among the vacant pulpits even there?

"How are you today?"

So it was one more pitch. Now was the time to cut Mr. Partridge off.

Nevertheless, Andrews made the fatal response. He answered, "Fine."

"You having pleasant weather up there today, Pastor?"

"Not too bad." A bad habit that came with the ministry was trying to be polite to everybody. Which served no charitable end.

"Nice weather down here, too." The quality of Gaylord's voice said that he had negotiated a narrow pass. He would march forward now across an open plain.

"Well, Pastor Andrews, I'd like to give you a chance to preview on video cassette one of the most inspiring motion pictures of all time. It's called *Glory on Death Row*. Maybe you've heard of it."

"I can't say that I have."

"I just thought someone might have told you about it, Pastor. The news travels fast on this one. The fact is, though, that *Glory on Death Row* is made available exclusively by True Word of God Studios, and it's just this week that the Lord has empowered us to reach out into your area. Pastor, this movie has in it actual members of the Bonnie and Clyde gang as well as—"

"You mean that some of them are still around?" He could not help himself. He had to ask.

"Actually, Pastor Andrews, I believe that part uses clips from the 1930s. But there's also more up-to-date footage with members of the Charles Manson family, people from the Watergate conspiracy, that young lady who was involved with Senator Hart, and right up to—"

"Quite a celebrated cast."

"It sure is." The voice was rising with enthusiasm. "You'll love it, Pastor Andrews. In fact, the story is built around George Hawkins. You must remember him."

"I can't say that I do."

"That's surprising, Pastor, because he was in the news quite a bit two, three years ago. George Hawkins, whom I can say I've met personally, praise the Lord, killed his mother-in-law with a curtain rod and then three other people. He was convicted of first degree murder and sentenced to die in the gas chamber and then, while he was on death row, Pastor Andrews, he found the Lord!"

"It sounds pretty miraculous."

"It is. But no man's past redeeming. Think of the thief on Calvary."

"What I meant was killing that many people with a curtain rod."

For perhaps five seconds, Gaylord Partridge was silent. Then he said in tones more subdued, "It was his mother-in-law he struck with a curtain rod. I couldn't say as to the others."

"Well, it doesn't matter," Andrews said. "But as to previewing this movie, right now, Gerald, I have a lot of things—"

"It's Gaylord, Pastor, Gaylord Partridge. Oh, you'll want to see this one. I didn't tell you that the governor commuted George's sentence on the grounds he was insane at the time. Between you and me, Pastor Andrews, I think what happened was, he was possessed by an evil spirit."

"Could be." He had to get this over with.

"But George is doing the Lord's work now in the state hospital, which is where I've had more than one inspiring conversation with him."

"You spend quite a bit of time there then?"

"Quite a bit, yes, Pastor. But wait till you see this video. I know you'll agree that *Glory on Death Row* is a real blockbuster. It's truly a spiritual presentation, not like some of these commercial movies made for the church market that are full of secular humanism in disguise."

"I can see that, Gaylord, but—"

"Pastor Andrews, do you have a sixteen-millimeter movie projector at your church?"

"Yes, we do, but—"

"We can let you have the full-length movie version in authentic color for only two hundred and twenty-five dollars."

Now he would end it!

"I'm sorry, but we're not in a position to buy any films right now."

"Well, then, Pastor, why not acquire the video for only seventy-nine ninety-five? Did I tell you that Horace Vanderberg is the chief narrator?"

"Horace Vanderberg?"

"I'm sure you've heard of him. He was a missionary to Borneo, and, while he was there, an exotic insect bit him."

"I can't say I recall . . ."

Awe hung in dark plumes from the man's voice. "Pastor, Horace Vanderberg was declared clinically dead for seventeen minutes!"

"That's amazing, but I've got people in my congregation, Gaylord, who've been clinically dead for seventeen years."

"Oh ho, Pastor Andrews. Now I know what you mean! And that's why you need this video. If anything will wake them up, it's *Glory on Death Row*."

"That may be. But I'm going to have to hang up now and go on to other things. Thanks for letting me know—"

"Pastor, why don't I just send you our mini-preview tape to look at? There's no obligation so long's you return it in twenty days. You can show it to your board and—"

"My board won't be meeting for another couple of weeks, and, in any case, this isn't the sort of church that goes in for movies like that. I really think you're wasting—"

"When does your board meet exactly?"

"Tenth of next month."

"Fine, Pastor. I'll have the mini-preview video out there in time for your meeting, and along about November twelfth I'll give you a call."

"If you wish, but as I say, our church doesn't go in much for movies or videos."

"I understand, Pastor. So many corrupting things out there. But you just wait until your board sees this one. Well, now, I won't keep you any longer. The Lord bless you."

"And you, too."

It was the third call like that in a week. There was a time when such a call would not have happened. Gaylord would have known better than to call someone like Andrews. But now the Gaylords just assumed that everybody shared the same tastes. They were the new mainline Christians, after all.

The silence settled in. Andrews became aware of the

darkness. He had made his way to the phone on his desk without stopping to put on any lights. Not that he needed them. He could move through every room in the building blindfolded. But he reached for the desk lamp and turned it on. For a moment he contemplated the knotty pine paneling that had been installed by the men's club just before he began his pastorate in New Sharon. There had been quite a bit of correspondence about it before he arrived. There was a faction that wanted to paint the walls blue, and another that advocated wallpaper with fleur-de-lis. But he had encouraged the paneling cadre, and he was glad. They had used real boards, not the thin phoney stuff sold at home maintenance centers.

Andrews had always admired the pine paneling of Dr. Longworth's study in the big church back home. There was a real elegance about that room, with its row of bookshelves, great mahogany desk, and Chippendale chairs. The little study at New Sharon was less impressive, but when he first took possession of it, Andrews felt that he had achieved at last a true pastoral identity. The four walls, darkened with time, had become so much a part of him that it seemed his soul must be paneled with the same lumber. On those rare occasions when he tried to write a sermon somewhere else, the image of the knotty pine backdrop always came to mind.

He walked into the secretary's office, switching on the overhead light. Near the door leading to the hallway was the grid of pigeon-holes into which Millie put the sorted mail. There were about a dozen openings, marked variously Trustees, Dorcas Society, Treasurer, Pairs and Spares. The one marked Pastor was at the top, on the left. He could see that, as usual, his was full of third-class mail—advertisements for stoles, mimeographed notices of ecclesiastical gatherings.

Reaching into the hole, he lifted out the whole mass and carried it back to his study. He sat, not behind his desk, but in the one comfortable chair. His fingers came quickly to the only first-class item: the same envelope he had seen atop Millie's desk as he had passed by on his way to the Upsall funeral. Quickly, ruthlessly, he tore open the envelope and let it drop to the floor. He opened the letter. His eyes required only a sliver of a second to take in the gist: . . . *very much impressed with your gifts and abilities* . . . *with every good wish for your continuing ministry* . . .

He crumpled the letter into a ball and threw it across the room. It landed in one of the flower pots on the window sill, but he did not care. He did not care about anything. Could it be that he had arrived at last at that holy nonchalance that true saints attain? His soul was detached. It had come loose from his life.

He stood up. There were still things to set right. He would attend to the lights left burning in the empty building.

Passing through the narthex, he stumbled over two large sprays of mums and gladioli. He had told Young Greene, only one, but funeral directors were always looking to get rid of leftover flowers. One by one he carried the sprays into the galley kitchen off the parlor and placed the papier-mâché urns into the sink. He found a pitcher in the cabinet and doused the flowers with water. By Sunday the blooms would have wilted. For now he would put things right.

He was reaching for the sanctuary light switch when he was accosted by a banner:

Behold,

I

Make

All Things

New!

The banner stated the church theme for the program year. The youth group was to have made it at the retreat the previous Saturday, and here it was, in baby blue felt against a background of bright orange. He had expected them to hang it to one side, over the piano. Instead, they had suspended their banner above the choir loft from the nail used annually to hang the large Christmas wreath. He had installed that nail himself under the supervision of the flower committee.

He had no thought of moving the banner. The sentiment of youth must prevail. Otherwise, no telling what mischief they might get into. Not even the Dorcas ladies would dare protest the banner's confrontation with the crimson carpeting of the chancel and the aisles. The banner was askew, though, and that could be corrected.

Striding down the center aisle, Andrews went up into the choir loft, mounted one of the chairs, and tugged at the lower right corner of the banner in an effort to right it. Each effort at adjustment failed, however; as soon as he let go, the banner returned to the same crooked angle. It was evident that the correction could not be made from below, an observation which, had he been in the mood for it, might have prompted an excursus into theology. But he was not in the mood. What was required was that the wire holding the banner be moved an inch or so along the nail. He removed his overcoat and suit jacket and lay them across a pew. He then went down to the basement in search of a stepladder. The ladder was not in the custodian's closet where it belonged. But he would find it. He turned toward the assembly room and looked at his watch. Everything squandered his time. But he would find the ladder. The banner would be put right.

He spied the ladder standing on the stage. He carried it up the stairs and all the way to the rear of the choir loft. After he opened the ladder, he found it hard to establish a secure footing. He wondered how he had ever hammered the nail up there in the first place. Of course, he had been ten years younger at the time. He imagined the organist coming to practice and finding the Reverend Mr. Andrews lying unconscious beside the console.

Still, he managed to climb and descend the ladder several times. After each adjustment of the wire along the nail, he would go out to the center aisle to take another sighting. Even a quarter of an inch the wrong way was enough to make the entire room look awry. Finally he was satisfied that the banner came down at an angle as nearly perpendicular to the earth as mortal hands might achieve. When the sun streamed in the east windows, the bright orange backing would contend fiercely with the aisle runners. But the letters would look level. That much, at least, he had made right with the world.

He turned off the lights and stood for a moment in near total blackness. Then the headlights of a car flashed against one of the stained glass windows, sending him back again to those days in Foster when he used to go into the little frame church and preach his sermon to the darkness on Saturday nights.

After those practice sessions, he would walk down Main Street, passing along the two commercial blocks, looking into the shops and insurance offices. Everything would be open. The farmers and their families would all be in town. Sometimes he would greet people he knew. Most of the time he would just observe. The town was most alive on Saturday nights. He thought of himself as taking its pulse. When he reached the grain elevator, he would turn around and walk up the street on the other side toward the church, which stood on a slight rise and looked back at him darkly above a row of dying elms.

All of that was part of his routine, perhaps a ritual. He observed many rituals in those days, believing that he was disciplining himself for great achievements.

He returned the stepladder to the custodian's storage closet, a procedure that required the rearrangement of several mops and a stack of toilet paper. He looked at his watch again. It was seven thirty-five. Kate would be beside herself wondering what had happened to him. But there was something else undone. He stared at the black and white triangles of the hallway floor trying to remember. The tiles gave him vertigo. He reached for the wall. Then it came to him: the light in the ladies' restroom. If he failed to turn it off, some member of the board of trustees was bound to drive by, see the light shining, and complain about the waste. Something else for which the pastor would take the blame. A defect in his management. Andrews knew just which light had been left on: the one over the dressing table mirror that had its own separate switch. He put it right.

Behold,

I

Make

All Things

New!

Too late.

He would do his job in New Sharon for another two or three years and then retire. He owed it to the church not to stay too long. If, like Saul, he had lost the Spirit, he ought to leave before an evil spirit took over.

The trouble was that the earlier he retired, the smaller his pension would be. And aside from Social Security, he would not have much else. He and Kate had never owned a home of their own. They always lived in church residences. They had no equity in any property, not even a vacation cabin, and little savings. The small inheritances that each had received had largely been spent on their children's education.

He supposed he might spend a few years with another congregation somewhere. There were a lot of little churches

173

in need of help. If he searched hard enough, he would find one. He might even find something in Florida or the Southwest and get away from the cold. Of course, everybody was vying for those positions, so the competition was keen. Or he might do a series of interim ministries for larger churches that were between pastors. That might prove exciting, or at least offer frequent changes of scene. But he and Kate would need to have a home of their own somewhere if he were to travel around. Maybe he would need some special training for interim ministry. Younger clergy, people with no regular pastoral experience who could not find full-time jobs, were attending workshops and then getting certified for interim ministry positions. He would have to do that, too, despite his years of experience.

One way or another, he could postpone receiving his pension and Social Security until his monthly payments reached a higher level. He would get in touch with the pension board and the Social Security office and try to obtain estimates of what he would receive at different ages—not a very idealistic motivation for serving the church. But then, maybe the church owed him something. He was beginning to feel that it did.

Kate had some pension money coming, but not much. It was only recently that she had worked full time. In the early years, the congregations would not have approved. The parson's wife was meant to be a model of domesticity while, at the same time, serving as first lady of the church and filling in when needed for the education and music programs. As time went on, attitudes began to change, especially in a relatively large town such as New Sharon. When Kate took a full-time position at the high school to help pay for their children's college expenses, some of the ladies in the church seemed positively proud of her accomplishment. When the school budget crunch came along, Kate, who lacked seniority, was reduced to substituting at the middle school. The high school wanted her back again, but she wasn't enthusiastic about returning. Andrews wasn't sure why. He had the feeling that Kate wasn't happy in New Sharon. Perhaps now that their children were grown, she wanted the chance to live in a place where there was more to do and where there were more interesting people to talk to. It was hard for her to make friends in New Sharon. The women with similar interests tended to have much more money. And she was always the pastor's wife. It was a station in life that precluded intimacy.

One thing Andrews knew: he didn't want Kate working when he wasn't. He supposed he was as old-fashioned as most of the people in his congregation. But that was one inherited attitude he could not slough off. If Kate did decide to go back to teaching full time, he would have to keep working as long as she did.

The phone was ringing again. All lights off below, he ran up the stairs and picked up the telephone at the secretary's desk.

"Jack?"

Kate. She sounded worried. He never did consider her enough.

"Are you coming home sometime soon?"

"In just a minute."

"Mabel Schatz called. She said there was some sort of accident."

"Nothing serious. Boy in a pickup ran into one of the funeral cars. The boy was shaken up a little, I guess. The burial got sidetracked for a while."

"I wish I'd known. I had dinner all ready. I suppose you won't want any now."

No consideration at all. He said, "I did have a little to eat at the Ramseys' house. But I haven't really had dinner. You can warm something up for me."

"All right. And you'll be right home?"

"Yes."

He thought she was hanging up the phone. Instead, she asked, "Is everything all right?"

"Just a few lights to put out. I'll be right home."

He was in the pastor's study again to switch off the light there, too. After that, nothing but outer darkness. But something else was awry. The crumpled letter lay on the African violet in the window sill. There were six plants at his windows: two begonias, a white geranium, the African violet, and two others he could not name. He loved the nameless ones best. His Old Testament professor—"Old Negeb," they called him—used to say that nothing had being until Adam gave it a name. But then as now Andrews rebelled at the thought. He believed that Adam's giving things names was bound up with original sin. The label took the life away.

In any case, Andrews could not leave that ball of paper

on the African violet. When Millie went in to water the plants, she would remove the paper and quite likely she would read it. Andrews retrieved the letter, unraveled it, and looked at it again. There was something he had not noted at first. There was a handwritten postscript:

*Sorry. You would have made us a good pastor.*
*Best of luck,*
*Jim*

Too late.

Andrews crumpled the letter again and stuffed it into one of his pants pockets. He deferred the decision as to whether he would throw the letter in the parsonage trash or stick it in his personal file.

For the last time that day, the church phone was ringing.

"Hello, Revner Andrews?"

The voice sounded familiar, but he could not place the name.

"This is Mabel, Revner. Is that you? Your voice sounds kind of strange."

He cleared his throat. "I think it's me, Mabel. Your voice puzzled me at first, too. Maybe it's the connection."

"Maybe. That was a real nice funeral you had for Howard Upsall. Real nice. Everyone I talked to said so."

"Well, it's nice of you, Mabel, to let me know."

"Not at all, Revner. Not at all. People should know when they're appreciated. By the way, I called Kate to let her know about the accident and all. I was afraid she might be worrying, and I knew you wouldn't have much chance to phone her."

"Thanks. I appreciate that." Was there something else on her mind? It was a risk, but he asked, "What can I do for you?"

"Nothing much, Revner. I just thought I'd catch you since you wasn't home. A rumor's been going around that you might be leaving us."

"Oh?" He cleared his throat again. "It's best not to place stock in rumors, Mabel."

She chuckled. "You're right about that. But I understand some church out of state made inquiries about you. At least, that's what I've been told."

"Right. Churches do that sort of thing sometimes. But I'm still here, you see. I've no plans to move right now."

When Mabel spoke again, her voice was very low, almost a whisper. "Jack, I'm glad. We know you're entitled to bigger and better things. But you're needed here."

She hung up.

Andrews left the church and began navigating his way among the obstacles in the playground toward the back porch of the parsonage. The outside light was shining, beckoning to him. But there were dark passages to negotiate before he arrived at the steps. Through a window he could see Kate's shadow flickering along the dining room wall. More than once he had told her that he believed he could recognize her by shadow alone.

As if to confirm his belief, Kate herself appeared in the

window. She would notice that all the lights were off in the church and conclude that, at last, he was on his way home. Andrews watched her turn from the window and disappear in the direction of the kitchen. He supposed that she was going to take his dinner out of the oven one last time.

He just managed to skirt the sandbox. Again, Kate's shadow passed along the far wall of the dining room. He could see her standing under the arch. Something was in her hand. She was holding one of the silver candlesticks he had given her for their twenty-fifth wedding anniversary. It still held the red candle from last Christmas. Kate lighted the candle and placed the candlestick on the dining room table.

Andrews wondered what inspired this bit of ceremony. Did she think there was an occasion for celebration? Or was she trying to cheer him in the wake of bad news? He could think of no way she could have learned of the letter. But then, Kate always seemed to know everything about him. Whatever the reason for the candle, he was gladdened by it.

Recently, Andrews had fallen into reveries in which he imagined Kate in a new home, a home of their own, in one of the residential neighborhoods Jim Purdy had shown him. He had pictured Miriam visiting there with her husband and little boy. Bill was there, too, having come all the way from San Jose to see the new house.

For an instant, Kate appeared in the window again. She was on watch. As soon as she heard his step on the back porch, she would be at the door to meet him. He wanted to creep into the house like a sick dog and hide somewhere. But Kate would intercept him, as she had intercepted him many times before.

A storm of emotion broke within Andrews. He stifled a sob and reached out for one of the bars of the jungle gym, misjudged the distance, and stumbled. He was aware of that high eye of laughter looking down from within. After all, he had run into such obstacles before. He caught hold of the bar and steadied himself. In a moment, he went forward again.